I0534469

Make Me Immortal

BOOK 3

GINGER LEE

Copyright © Ginger Lee 2024

All rights reserved. No portion of this book may be used or reproduced in any form without permission from the author, except as permitted by U.S. copyright law.

No AI was used for any of the writing or creation of this book.

This book is a work of fiction. Names, characters, businesses, organizations, places, events and incidents either are the product of the author's imagination or are used fictitiously.

Editor Brandi Zelenka

My Notes in the Margin

www.mynotesinthemargins.com/

Cover design by Angela Haddon

Cover Photographer Christopher John

CJC Photography

www.cjc-photography.com/

Printed in the United States of America

Paperback ISBN 979-8-9885489-1-1

Ebook ISBN 979-8-9885489-2-8

Author's Website: www.gleewrites.com

 Created with Vellum

Make Me Immortal

GINGER LEE

One

I thought it would be nice to have some normalcy back in my home after everyone had left, but I found it a bit lonely. I even missed the bloody witches. Especially Willa. Saying goodbye and watching her board the Invictus was the hardest thing I've ever had to do, but I knew I would see her again in my dreams.

DAVID

Feathery fingertips brushed my lips, bringing me to life. The weight of Willa on my chest felt like heaven on earth and my arms wrapped her up, wishing she would stay with me forever. It had only been a week since she had gone back to New Orleans but it felt like an eternity to my longing immortal soul. Willa kissed me softly and my heart beat faster.

"My wild one," she whispered.

"I've missed you, babe." I rolled her over, pinning her underneath me.

"Has it been *hard* being here without me," she teased as she slid a hand down and grabbed my cock.

I growled, "Yes, you golden-haired minx."

She stroked up and down. "You know I told you to have fun at the club without me."

"I know. I'm sure I will...eventually, but I haven't been in the mood until now."

I nuzzled my nose behind her ear, taking in the scent of cinnamon spiced vanilla I would never get enough of. I kissed her sweet neck and her blood pumped against my tongue in the perfect place for a taste. She turned her head, offering herself as I sank in my fangs. She moaned and pushed my hips up with her hands then pulled them back down as I slipped inside, enveloped by her warmth. Willa's nails dug into my flesh and when her palms flattened on my skin, her energy vibrated. We had only played, teased, and pleasured one another before. This was the first time feeling her magic from the inside. Willa felt and tasted like heaven. I thrusted faster, harder, and sucked on her neck deeper as I edged myself and waited for her to come. She gasped before howling my name. The final sweet release was beyond satisfying. I had never orgasmed in unison with someone before and it was profoundly intimate.

I licked the wound and kissed her neck. Willa's voice buzzed against my lips when she spoke.

"Oh, god. That was so loud. I didn't mean to be so loud."

I laughed. "It doesn't matter. No one else is in the house. I quite fancied it."

"Mmm, good," she purred and surprised me by flipping us over to straddle my waist. "You ready for another go, then, my wild one?"

I sat up and grabbed her around the waist. "Time for round two!"

WILLA

I startled awake in my own bed between Alder and Micah feeling drugged. Astral projection took a tremendous amount of energy. I had a lot to learn about it. I spent a little longer with David than I had anticipated, because I wasn't sure how often I would be able to visit. I had already spoken with Alder and Micah about David spending time in New Orleans only two days after leaving London. Alder surprised me by suggesting David buy property in the Garden District near our home, so we could have privacy when he made the trip over.

I stretched and curled myself around Alder from behind. He sighed, kissed my hand, and tucked it under his chin. I let my foot touch Micah's and when he realized I had returned to the bed, he flipped over and spooned me. His hand found my breast and he hummed.

"We're like an Oreo and you're the cream," he joked sleepily.

"A whoreo, if you will," I retorted.

We giggled like teenagers.

"Ha! Whoreo. You should do stand-up, Willa," Micah said sarcastically. I elbowed his hard abdomen, which hurt my funny bone and had absolutely no effect on him.

"Owww," I exclaimed.

"Behave, you two," Alder scolded. "You're no match for us, Willa."

I propped my head on Alder's shoulder. "Well, I will be soon."

He pulled my arm tighter around himself. "Someday."

He knew I had already been considering being turned. He didn't think I was ready. Maybe I wasn't, but it sure would make me feel safer after everything that we had been through lately. Like I didn't need so much protecting from my mates.

"We want to protect you," Micah replied to my thoughts. He was getting better at reading my mind. Alder said drinking my blood enhanced the ability. "You are powerful too Willa," Micah reminded me.

Alder turned his body over to face me and looked deep into my eyes. His shined. He slowly slid his fingers through my hair. "I'm honestly nervous about you becoming one of us. What power will you hold then?"

Micah propped up over my shoulder, listening to Alder's serious tone. I sighed. "Do you think I could become something dangerous?"

Alder kissed me sweetly before answering. His nose nuzzled mine. I knew he was thinking about what to say. "I'm not sure. There is a small chance that the true vampire ego, which can be vicious, may battle to dominate your personality. Us vampires have to keep our egos in check. Cateline didn't want anyone to have what she couldn't. I guess the same goes for witches. Wesley wanted to rule the world. The ego takes over and they feel unstoppable. I've never heard of a true vampire witch, but I promise I won't let the actions of others shadow over what you could be."

I stretched onto my back between them. "Too bad vampires can't tell the future the way you can read thoughts."

"You sort of can," Micah reminded me.

"Yeah, but that hasn't happened in so long. And it was only one night in advance before a client's appointment and pretty specific to a single situation. Anyway, I haven't dreamt about any damn thing since all of this astral projection fuckery has begun. *Not* that I'm complaining about easily being able to see David," I laughed.

Alder laid a hand on my abdomen. "Maybe that's because you're always sleeping between two vampires. Would you want your own room back?"

Micah looked worried that I would say yes. Alder's hand left me and reached for Micah's face. "Willa might need some space. Alone time may seem like a small thing to us vampires, because we have it in abundance, but it is important to humans."

I touched Micah's other cheek. "I don't want you out of my bed. Not at all."

He smiled. "Good."

Alder got up and started to get dressed. "My place here is small. I don't have an extra room, but I'll look for something a bit larger for David. I think we should set up a nice space for you at his place when you need some time to decompress."

I sat up. "That sounds perfect."

WILLA

After hearing that Alder was looking for the perfect property that David and I could both use, Trace took it upon herself to begin the search. She sat at the kitchen island intently scrolling on her laptop. I peeked over her shoulder.

"Ooo, look at this one." She clicked on the photo gallery. "You know, I'm only searching within a mile radius."

I laughed. "Oh, I'm not surprised one bit."

"Willa, we've been together our whole lives. I hope you understand the need to keep you close. I hope David understands that his options are limited and our requirements for a place are more important than his," she joked.

I set down my coffee mug and put my arms around her shoulders. "We are soul sisters. Our vampires are going to have to deal with that. You and I are a package deal."

Trace squeezed my arm then continued scrolling. Alder and Micah walked in, and Trace called Alder over to look at a couple of listings.

Micah beamed when the doorbell rang. "That will be for me."

He returned to the kitchen carrying four boxes stacked on top of one another and set them on the counter. They were black and simply said *Vena* in a gothic red font.

"Oh, brilliant. It's here," Alder said.

Micah put two boxes in the pantry and the others in the fridge next to Trace's boxed wine. He grabbed two glasses and filled them with the spout then handed one to Alder.

"Well, that's convenient," I said. "How does it stay fresh? Does it even taste good cold?"

Alder hummed. "Mmm, yes. I've invested heavily in this new company. I'm not sure how they do it, but this is a game changer for us vampires." He swirled the dark liquid in his glass. "This will be huge. Our scientists are working on a coffee brand as well. They are getting the flavor just right."

"Bloody good coffee," Micah joked in his best British accent.

"That's a cracking accent mate," Harris said as he joined us.

"It's also a great name," Alder added.

I laughed. "It really is." I tapped the mug I retrieved from the upper cabinet, distracted by a thought. "A coffee shop," I blurted out.

I stood behind Alder. "I know you don't want to open a club like Lust, but what about a vampire coffee shop?"

Trace gasped. "What about a witchy vampire coffee shop? Oh my gosh, I could do tarot readings a few nights a week!"

Alder and Harris looked at each other. Harris kissed the top of Trace's head. "Brill, darlings. Amazing, you two. I want in."

Alder smiled. "I think the clutch would love this. Humans, too. It's a smashing way to bring everyone together. Alright, Trace, add a retail building to your real estate search."

She looked at me. "So. When's David coming here for a visit?"

I sighed and shrugged. "I'm not sure." There was a lot more I wanted to say to her. As witches, we understood each other better than the vampires would. I had a lot of deep feelings and emotional pull coming from David. Even being so far away.

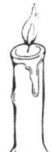

Two

DAVID

I had become a depressed vampire. As soon as Willa disappeared, my heart ached. I became irritable and moody and I'm sure Marco felt it. She was so far away. I forced myself out of my room and walked down the hall. Marco stood in the front doorway, looking out into the dark. "What the fuck are you doing?"

He turned and rolled his eyes. "Settle down, try to relax and pull out whatever's climbed up your ass."

I scoffed and joined him at the door. I sniffed the air. "Really, what's up?"

"William is on his way. I asked him to arrive a little earlier than normal tonight. He's going with you when you go to the States. He just doesn't know it yet."

"I don't need a chaperone."

"Don't argue with me, David. You may be the primus of the clutch here, but I can't go with you. You're used to Will acting as your bodyguard around London anyway. And with all the drama that's been going on lately, we're not taking any chances."

I sighed and patted his shoulder. "Alright, mate." Just then I saw the huge gray wolf leap up and over the high iron gate with ease. Will shook his fur like a wet dog as he went from all fours to standing erect, now in his naked human form. He sauntered over and took the clothes Marco held out to him.

"Hey, boss. Marco." He nodded to us both and we followed him inside. He dressed in the kitchen and Marco dished him up his favorite shepherd's pie. Will had, for the most part, stayed away while the witches were around. Not many humans were aware that shapeshifters actually existed. Will had been born into his lineage from old Romania. Protection agreements between vampires and shifters began there long ago. Vampires had been taught the legend of Vlad III keeping an entire pack with him at castle Poenari and were still encouraged to form alliances with local packs. Wherever vampires ventured, shifters weren't far behind. I wasn't sure if they took any other animal forms, but I knew the trait had to be passed down. I had never asked Will about any other species.

"I know it's nothing unusual for me to be over for dinner, but you said there was something we needed to discuss?"

Marco spoke up. "Do you have any plans for the next couple of weeks?"

"Nothing I can't rearrange. What's up?"

"Fancy a trip to New Orleans with me?" I asked.

Will downed a bottle of beer. "Are we going to see Willa?"

Gold sparkled in his dark brown eyes at the idea and the corner of his mouth turned up. It figured that he was attracted to her. I couldn't blame him. She was beautiful and her energy made creatures of every kind want to be in her orbit.

"We are and I would feel safer with you there. Besides, Marco insists."

Marco laughed and took Will's plate for seconds. Will never left a crumb. His appetite was definitely all wolf.

"Thank you, Marco. I haven't been out of London in a good while. Sounds perfect."

I was relieved. "They will be resting right now, but I'll let Alder know the plan."

WILLA

"Are you sure Will won't mind sleeping in my parlor? I'm surprised he's not staying at the same hotel as David." Alder and I tucked a fitted sheet over the mattress of a temporary twin bed Trace and I brought down from the attic.

"Well, since Micah is no longer human, Will can help keep the place a little more secure during the day while they are here."

We spread a cozy quilt on top and I went to Alder and wrapped my arms around his waist. He grabbed onto me and threw us both onto the bed, sprinkling kisses all over my face. I held onto him so tight. "Let's stay here forever," I said wistfully. I meant it. I would be content eclipsed by Alder.

He nuzzled his nose behind my ear and whispered, "We may be able to fit Micah on this tiny bed with us."

I sighed. I loved how he thought of us as a unit. I reluctantly pushed Alder off and sat up. "It would be rude to have sex on these clean sheets before our house guest gets here," I joked.

We straightened the covers, and I began anxiously awaiting David's arrival.

DAVID

My slow beating heart soared when Willa suggested I get a flat in New Orleans. Of course I would. I needed her now, and being an immortal vampire, the trips back and forth would seem like fleeting moments. Especially when I planned on using that time to rest. I was sure Will, on the other hand, would soon grow tired of the journey. I was used to having protection in London, but the Hunt clutch didn't do things the same way. At least, not that I was aware of. That was something I needed to discuss with Will later. I wondered if he had any relatives I could trust in the States who would offer their services.

I finally took a deep breath when we pulled up next to Alder's Jag at Trace and Willa's Garden District home. I had texted Willa when we landed and she was sitting on the porch, waiting for me. It was dark and the windows of the black SUV were tinted, so I knew she couldn't see the huge smile on my face. I was out and had scooped her up within seconds. My arms went around her waist and I squeezed her and twirled her around. "Babe." Willa laughed and then sighed, and I kissed her. Our lips were locked together. My fangs descended and my tongue slid over hers. She moaned and I grunted. She smelled and tasted so good. My mate. We heard Will clear his throat after a minute or two and Willa pulled back to peer over my shoulder.

"Oh, hello, William," she said meekly.

I turned to see his face flushed with either embarrassment or his own lustful thoughts. I had never been able to read Will's mind. It must have been a shifter thing.

"Hello, Ms. Deberry."

She let go of me and went over to him. "You better call me Willa. Ms. Deberry makes me feel old."

Will actually batted his eyelashes and grinned down at her. "I'd never want to make you feel like that." He touched her arm. "Thank you for opening up your home to me. I promise I'll behave." He winked and I swear Willa swooned.

I was surprised he showed any feelings of attraction for her right in front of me. They kept eye contact. She stood very close, her head tilted up to his face since she was a good foot shorter, and it was like they were entranced. I put my hands on Willa's shoulders to bring them out of it. I raised my eyebrows at him. "You'll have to thank Trace as well. Let's get your luggage, shall we?"

WILLA

I shook my head and led David and Will into the house. *What the hell was that? What am I doing? Holy shit, David can read my mind. Clear your thoughts, Willa. For fucks sake, clear your thoughts.* The heated buzz running through my body was betraying me. Alder could read me better than anyone and when our eyes met, his looked mischievous with amusement over my very obvious flustered state.

Everyone had gathered in the kitchen and were saying their hellos. Micah kissed my forehead then went back to cooking dinner. I busied myself and my mind by getting wine for us humans. Trace passed out glasses of the new boxed blood to the vampires. I stood at the stove next to Micah while the others chatted. He hip bumped me. "What's going on?"

I shrugged. "Huh? Nothing. What do you mean?"

He offered me a taste of the pesto sauce. "Mmm. So good."

He went back to stirring. "I know you. There's a lot going on in that head of yours."

I emptied my glass. "Maybe." I played coy, but he was right. He knew me very well. I noticed Micah glance at Will, who was laughing at something Trace had said, but he didn't look at her the way he looked at me. I set my mouth into a straight line. "I'm not sure what the universe is trying to do, but it's all getting to be a bit much, right? These next few days are supposed to be about me and David spending some quality time together." I leaned my head on Micah's shoulder and whispered, "Why the fuck do I feel like I just bonded with Will?"

Micah flipped the gas stove knobs off and turned to everyone enthusiastically. "Time to eat!"

I scoffed at him and mouthed, *you aren't helping me, are you?* He smiled. "Nope."

Micah made plates while I poured myself more wine. I needed to focus on David. He came all the way here for me and I sincerely couldn't wait to get him alone. Our time together during astral projection was amazing, but the feelings of it being a dream always lingered. I grabbed the last serving of pasta and went to my seat next to David. I could feel Will's eyes on me. Did anyone else notice? I didn't look his way but leaned my shoulder against David's. He smiled and I kissed him sweetly to prove a point.

Thankfully, conversation came easily, and I pushed away intrusive thoughts about Will, but my nerves were antsy to leave and go to the hotel with David. He hadn't shown a lot of affection out of respect for Alder and Micah.

After dinner, I said goodbye to my mates and practically rushed David out the front door.

"Willa are you okay?" he asked as I trotted down the porch steps to my Jeep. I stopped abruptly when I heard Will's voice.

"You good, boss?" He stood on the stoop. His eyes were on me again.

"Yeah, mate. You're off the clock for tonight."

"Bye, Will," I mumbled as I slammed the driver side door. I saw him watching us in the rearview as I pulled away. *Maybe I'm making it all up. Maybe he's just concerned for David's safety.*

Three

DAVID

Willa squirmed in her seat. I wasn't sure how she managed to concentrate on her driving. She was trying so hard to keep me from reading her mind. I reached over and took her hand. The intense energy gave me a jolt much like when children scoot their socked feet across carpet on purpose and touch something metal for a shock. I rubbed my thumb into her palm.

"Relax, babe. I want you to teach me how to help ground you like Micah does." She didn't say a word.

We arrived at the hotel and Willa remained on edge until I pulled her into our suite and sat her on the end of the bed. I kneeled in front of her and laid my head on her lap. I heard her let out a deep breath and her hands were in my hair. "Mmm, Willa, I've missed you."

"I've missed you too, David."

I sat up to look into her eyes. "Is there something you want to tell me? You're trying so hard to not let me in. Have I done something?"

Her shoulders relaxed and she smiled. "Oh no. You...you are perfect. I..."

"You can tell me anything. You can't keep it all inside. You've never judged me, and I would never judge you." I put her hand on my heart. "Let me in."

"I will, but first..." Willa pulled my mouth to meet hers. Her lips and tongue were so soft. I couldn't get enough of her. I felt the rush of her emotions. She loved me and wanted to let me know this time was precious. She didn't want whatever was going on in her head to take away from our time together, but she didn't realize that I would stay. I would stay as long as she would have me. I would give up my place as the primus of the London clutch. I would lay down before her feet and offer my heart and immortal soul to be hers. But I would push all of my own thoughts down for now. Willa needed assurance that she could confess anything to me. We kissed madly and deeply, and I moved her up onto the bed and covered her with my body. She pulled my hips down, desperate to be as close as possible. I reached a hand between her legs to tease her. *Fuck.* Willa was wet through her leggings. I circled her clit and she panted.

"Oh, god. Don't stop."

I didn't dare. I couldn't. She needed release. My fingers moved faster, and she bucked up and called out my name as she came. I loved it when she called out my name.

"I want you. Now," she demanded.

I yanked the leggings down. Blimey, Willa wasn't wearing underwear. I jumped up, tore off my clothes, and pounced back on top. The tip of my cock parted her lips, and she was so slick, I slid in with a hard fast thrust. She sucked in a breath and her eyes were on fire.

"Again. Fuck me hard."

"Yes, babe." I went in again. Harder this time and she cried out. I picked up the pace. Faster. Harder. Her second orgasm hit, she clenched around my cock with otherworldly vibrations, and I exploded into a million pieces. Willa's legs were wrapped around me, and my head rested on her warm breasts. Her fingertips massaged my scalp and we both sighed.

When she finally spoke, her words came out nervously jumbled. "I'm just going to say it, because you're going to read my mind anyway, but Will and I had a moment after you arrived and I don't know what the hell it was, but it felt like a bond was formed. A strong one, and I'm not sure what it means, and it scares me."

I paused. Willa didn't know Will was a shifter, so the word bond scared me too. If he did indeed bond with her, it could mean a million different things and change our lives in a million different ways. And what the fuck would Alder and Micah think? Or do? My mind raced. Did Alder have any inclination that something happened? I propped up on one elbow and searched Willa's eyes.

"Is it that bad?" she asked. "Please don't be angry with me."

"No, no. I'm not angry. How could I be angry?" I thought fast and attempted to play it down. "You are so special. Your very existence pulls others into your orbit. Who doesn't want a connection with magic?"

She smiled. "You flatter me."

"Always," I vowed.

ALDER

When William left to go for a late-night run, I pulled Micah into Willa's bedroom to talk. He plopped down and stretched out on her bed like he had done a thousand times before, then patted the spot next to him. His eyebrows raised playfully. "We have it all to ourselves tonight."

He made me laugh, but I had to share what was on my mind. I sat beside him and held his hand. "We need to talk."

His mouth turned down and he sat up. "What's wrong? I feel like you're about to drop a bomb on me."

"No, Micah. We need to talk about Willa...and Will."

"You mean Willa and David?"

"Willa and Will."

He looked thoroughly confused.

"Have you ever heard of shifters?"

"In movies. Never in the real world, but I guess I believe anything is possible at this point."

"Well, they're human, but shift into animal form. It's a trait passed down through ancestral bloodlines. These humans have kept their secret well. Wherever there are vampires, you'll usually find shifters who act as protectors, and they are compensated well. But not here for some reason. I honestly don't know why, nor do I know all of the ins and outs of shifter and vampire relations, but in other countries, shifters offer protection to our kind, and we keep their secret. Will is a shifter. A wolf. I knew his father, Luca, in London. Luca and his wife live with David's business partner and former primus of the clutch, Ian."

"Does Willa know about any of this?"

I shook my head, "No. Nothing. I never bothered to mention it because New Orleans has been a peaceful home for us. Well, until the Cateline and Wesley fiascos. I guess that's why we never began the practice here. And vampires won't disclose it to humans. We are as loyal to them as they are to us. Will is David's protector."

"Holy shit. Willa mentioned having a moment with him earlier tonight. What does this mean?"

I got up and paced. "I'm not sure yet. I do know that when a shifter bonds to another, it's usually their mate. For life."

Micah stood to look me in the eyes. "What are we gonna do about it? It's gotta be a mistake, right?"

"I need to learn more. I need to talk to David."

There was a knock on the door. It was Will.

He peeked his head in and had his gym bag over one shoulder. "Trace said I could take a shower in here since Willa was gone for the night. Is this a bad time?"

I felt jealousy rise within me. My chest tightened and I was surprised. He was masculine and handsome and sweaty from head to toe from his run. "No, mate. Come on in."

Micah cleared his throat. "There are towels in the closet behind the door. We'll give you some privacy."

MICAH

I went straight to the upper kitchen cabinet that housed liquor and retrieved a bottle of Jack Daniels' Twice Barreled whiskey. Vampires metabolized alcohol slower than humans, so it took more to get a good buzz. I threw back half a tumbler and coughed. Alder took the empty glass and added ice to mine and his.

"Slow down, love."

"Damn, the man is good looking. What are you thinking? I'm jealous, Alder. If all of this is true, I don't like it. I'm just being honest."

He leaned on the counter and winked. "I'm a wee bit jealous too. We shouldn't let it show. Out of respect to David, we have to be nice. Will is a guest here. I'll speak with David later. I don't want to disturb them on his first night in town."

I nodded. "And Will is here with us, not Willa. Maybe we're making more of it than we should. I mean, can Willa handle another mate?"

I felt both of our hearts sink at the thought. What if it was true? Was Will destined to be in Willa's life? Who were we to stop the universe from carrying out its plan? We hated the idea. Hell, David would probably hate the idea as well.

Will walked into the kitchen and straight to the pantry. I went over, reached in front of him, and pulled out a bag of pasta. He smelled like Willa's body wash. "Want some dinner? I make a helluva great marinara."

"Yeah, that's brilliant. I'm bloody starving."

Alder laughed. "I forget you shifters can never get your fill."

Will froze, his eyes darting over to mine.

"Your secret is safe with Micah," Alder assured.

Will visibly relaxed. "Do the witches know?" He plucked grapes from a bowl on the island and stuffed them into his mouth.

Alder shook his head. "Not yet."

I started cooking and Harris and Trace joined us.

"Mmm, I smell spaghetti," Trace practically moaned as she peered over my shoulder.

"I'll let you taste test the sauce as soon as it's hot."

Harris handed me a glass of Vena. "Want me to slice the bread?"

"Yes, please."

"You all have quite the harmonious home here, don't you? It seems like everyone gets along and contributes. I've never seen vampires and witches together, much less in the same dwelling," Will said with admiration and genuine curiosity.

Trace leaned on the counter across from him and popped a grape into her mouth. "Believe me, we're just winging it."

Will leaned in closer to her. "Hey, would you have time while I'm in town to do a reading for me?"

Trace lit up. "Oh, yes. I'd love to."

Maybe, he was just a big flirt, I thought as I watched them. He did have a natural charm about him, and he was handsome as hell. Alder had been leaning on the counter right beside me and he gently elbowed my side. "He doesn't compare to you," he whispered with a wink. I swooned, but I knew he was just flattering me. Will could totally be a model.

"Okay, Trace. Is it ready?"

She slurped sauce from the wooden spoon I held out and her eyes rolled back. "Mmm, perfect."

Four

WILLA

I put on a robe and David dressed and ordered room service since I was a human and needed to eat. A box of Vena was on the cart when it was delivered to our room. I read aloud the note attached. "Enjoy! All my love, Alder."

"Well, that's thoughtful and very welcome," David said as he sat in a chair and patted his hungry stomach.

"He doesn't want you to drain me dry," I joked.

"And he wants to remind me who you belong to." David pulled me onto his lap and growled while kissing my neck. I moaned and got instantly wet. I panted and squirmed as his cock hardened under my bottom. His hand squeezed my ass and I felt like I was on the verge of an orgasm already. I found his eager mouth and sucked on his bottom lip. He gasped and grinded his hips up against me.

I stopped him. "Wait."

His eyes went wide, but he didn't say a word. David remembered. He knew I was in control. He wanted me in control, even if it pained him physically to slow down. His biggest turn on was delayed gratification and I loved playing the game. I stood up, poured Vena into a glass, and handed it to him. He adjusted his boxer briefs with a big sigh, and a wicked smile on his lips. I sat

19

across from him and drizzled honey on a bran muffin. It was delicious. I hadn't realized how much I needed to eat.

I needed to calm down as well. I nearly came when I crossed my legs. I swiped a finger into the pooled honey on my plate and offered it to him. He leaned over and licked it with fire in his eyes, but still said nothing as he adjusted himself again.

"More?"

David nodded.

"Say please."

"Please."

I stood in front of him and slid one shoulder of my robe down to expose my breast. I ached for him. He waited. Then I drizzled the thick sweet amber liquid over one nipple. I burned with desire. He waited. I grasped the back of his head and invited his mouth to partake. He lapped and sucked and tugged with his teeth. I took his wrist and directed his hand where I wanted it to go. Yes. Right there. My head fell back when his fingers slipped between my folds and his thumb circled my clit. I was panting again, and David rubbed harder. I felt fangs scrape my skin and my knees came together, keeping his hand where it was as I writhed against it, coming hard and fast. I wanted more. I turned around, lifted the robe up, and bent over.

"Spank me."

He obeyed with a smack, but I needed more.

"Again. Harder."

He slapped my ass hard, and I heard him growl.

"Bite me, David. Taste me."

His hands gripped my hips and fangs sank into my buttock as I let out a scream. "Yes. Yes, David. Take it. Take me."

The sucking sounds turned me on again and I was ready to be fucked. "Stop. It's time. I need you."

He didn't hesitate for a second. He scooped me up and threw me down on the bed. I smiled and my body vibrated with anticipation. He undressed, hard and ready but stood still, waiting for me. "Take the rest of me, my wild one."

I expected David to pounce on top, slam into me, and be done quickly. Wham bam thank you ma'am. He surprised me. The light in his eyes flickered. He smiled and ran his tongue over his fangs. Then he climbed on hands and knees and stopped, hovering over me as he leaned down and took in my scent. His nose barely skimming the skin along my neck, clavicle, and abdomen. He gently placed a single kiss above my bellybutton before holding my wrists above my head, pressed against the mattress, and settling his body on mine. The act was completely erotic and feral. He used a knee to part my legs. I hooked them around his waist, and he slid inside. I throbbed and tightened around him. David kissed me slowly and moved in and out slower. It felt like time was standing still and I had gone to heaven. It felt like we would make love for eternity. Being together through astral projection was nothing compared to this.

David gradually increased his pace and grunted with each thrust. I couldn't wait any longer and sent the energy swirling within my chest down below. As soon as he felt the sensation, we came together. Perfection.

MICAH

I watched in amazement as Will ate three plates of pasta and an entire loaf of French bread.

"Thanks for leaving a little for me," Trace joked.

"Oh, shit. I'm sorry. I have a voracious appetite," he replied with a wink.

My god, everything about him oozed seduction. I shook my head, thinking about Willa feeling a bond with him, and Alder read my mind. He squeezed my thigh. *It's okay, love.*

After Will took his last bite, he hopped up and began clearing the plates. "I've got this. Thank you so much for the meal, Micah." He rinsed plates and Trace loaded the dishwasher. "Did you find a place for David yet?" he asked her. My senses perked up at his question.

Trace lowered her voice, but I could hear her. "Well, when I started the search, I was only looking in this neighborhood, but there's a perfect property not too far from here in Marigny. Especially since we are going to open a vampire coffee shop."

Will leaned closer. "Why are we whispering?"

"Because if we buy it, there's no need to keep this house, and I haven't told anyone that I'm thinking about selling. I mean, Harris knows. He can read my mind. And I know he and Alder would be fine with it, but Willa. I have no idea what Willa will say."

"If it's everything you all need…"

"Oh, I forget, you're new to us." Trace laughed. "Willa and I grew up here. I know it's sentimental to her. It is to me too, but I think I'm ready for the next chapter, you know?"

I sighed, listening to Trace speak with Will. Her grandmother's home was sentimental to me as well, but the thought of moving excited me. We did need a bigger space. Our family unit seemed to grow by the day. I got more Vena and joined them.

I winked at Trace to let her know I heard every word. "So, when are you going to show us this place?"

She rolled her eyes. "Holy shit, I can't keep anything from you guys, can I?"

Trace grabbed her laptop from her room, and we all went to the living room. Alder and I sat on either side of her. Harris stood behind the sofa to see the screen. Will sat on the edge of his temporary bed, listening to us.

"See? There are four separate living quarters, a courtyard, a small pool that needs a little TLC, and a space that's perfect for the coffee shop and tarot parlor. The building would be super easy to secure for you vampires."

She shifted the laptop to Alder's lap, and he scrolled through the photos. "Brilliant, Trace. I love the possibilities and the privacy, yet togetherness. You have been so gracious with your home, and it has been all you and Willa needed, but it is getting a little tight with all of us. I'll set up a tour for tomorrow night." He looked into Trace's eyes. "You're sure about this?"

She nodded. "As long as Willa feels good about it."

I smiled at her. "I seriously think she'll love it."

DAVID

My Willa. Well, she belonged to Alder, but when she was with me, she was all mine. The only woman to ever tame me. The only creature I craved. The thought of surrendering myself to one mate used to scare me. I'm a sexual being and have carefully dominated many women with extreme control. Almost every vampire eventually connects to and finds a forever mate, but I never envisioned it happening to me any time soon. And never considered the possibility of spending eternal life with a witch. A witch with two other mates.

But here Willa lay beside me. We had found pleasure in one another all night and slept all day. I woke just before dusk and stared at her. She stirred when I ran my hand down her arm and intertwined our fingers. Willa hummed, content. Her eyes blinked open, and I smiled. She pulled me closer and nuzzled into my chest. I wrapped her up, safe and secure.

"I'm so happy you're here, David," she whispered.

"Last night was the best night ever. Well, my birthday was pretty great too," I added.

Willa laughed. "Oh, yes. I quite enjoyed it myself." She stretched and yawned. "I'm going to freshen up. Will you have some coffee sent up, please?"

"Of course, babe."

We headed over to Willa's home when the moon shined high in the sky. Will was asleep but jolted awake as soon as I entered the house. His hearing was unbelievably better than a vampire's and he knew my scent. I patted his shoulder. "It's okay, mate. You can sleep as long as you like. We're all good."

He rubbed his sleepy eyes that were now set on Willa. His chest was bare, and he didn't attempt to cover himself. He usually slept nude and I hoped he was clothed under the quilt. Willa's attention was locked onto his and I had to touch her shoulder to break the trance. She looked away and went to the kitchen, following the smell of Trace's pancakes.

I stepped closer to Will. "Everything alright?"

"Yeah, boss. Why?"

"I see the way you look at her."

"It's nothing. I swear."

I only nodded. "Great then. Come eat or sleep longer if you want."

He got up, thankfully he had sleep pants on, and followed me to join the others.

Micah hugged Willa and lifted her off her feet to twirl her around. She giggled and he kissed her neck. Then, she peeled away to hold on to Alder who passionately kissed her on the lips. The scene was arousing, and I thought I could get used to this. I realized Willa was full of energy and had more than enough to give.

"I'll never make enough pancakes to fill you up," Trace joked while she stacked four on a plate. Will laughed and took it but offered it to Willa. She smiled meekly. "Thanks." Will blushed and I looked at Alder. He raised his eyebrows. *We should talk soon*, I let him know with my thoughts.

Hey, I want to be there when you do, Micah added to the inaudible conversation.

We all sat at the dining room table and Trace opened her laptop to show me and Willa the listing she found. It had separate apartments, including a large possible retail space.

Willa lit up. "Oh my gosh, Trace. Are you thinking what I'm thinking? I hope you're thinking what I'm thinking."

Trace bit her bottom lip nervously. "What are you thinking?"

Willa scrolled to a photo. "This. This is perfect for the coffee shop. It even has a room over here for the tarot readings and plenty of space for a coffee bar with couches and bookcases." She chose the pic of the floor plan. "One...two...three...four...Trace! We could all live here. Like all of us. How amazing would that be?"

Willa turned to me and touched my arm. "Wait. I mean, if everyone is on board with the idea, of course." Then she looked at Alder and then to Micah. They smiled.

"Trace? Are we on the same page?"

"Yes. Yes, wouldn't it be amazing?"

Willa's shoulders relaxed. "Phew. I was hoping I wasn't coming out of left field here. David, what do you think?"

I grabbed her hand and held it on my thigh. "I can't wait to see it, babe."

Five

WILLA

Alder, Micah, and Will rode with David in his rental car. Harris followed, driving my Jeep while Trace and I talked nonstop the entire way.

Esplanade Avenue would be an amazing location for both a vampire coffee shop and tarot parlor. The big brick building was u-shaped with wrought iron balconies on every side and a beautiful courtyard in the middle. There were a lot of windows, but we could easily add reinforced, blackout hurricane shutters for protection from the sunlight and security. As we walked onto the porch and into the huge open retail space, energy swelled up inside me. Micah came behind me and rubbed up and down my arms. His touch reminded me to take a deep breath and send some of the energy out through my feet. Trace spun around the room, taking it all in.

"Well, I think we can check this box off as amazing," Alder stated.

"Amazeballs," I corrected.

He laughed. "Yes, darling. Amazeballs."

I loved hearing him say it in his British accent.

We all meandered through the other four apartments. One was at the top of a staircase above the shop while the other three formed the u-shape of the courtyard around the pool. Each one had a kitchen opening to a living room, two bedrooms and two baths. Two units had additional spare rooms that could serve as offices. The real estate agent met us back where we started.

"Are there many offers yet," Alder asked.

"Not at 2.5 million, no. You all have time to discuss it. It has only been on the market a week, though, so I look forward to hearing from you soon."

Back at our home, Trace and I hugged while we walked up to the porch. She went inside with Harris, and I held David back. I looked up at him. His eyes smoldered with want, but I wouldn't move forward with any plans without his consent. "Tell me what you really think. I know you were expecting a place a little more private."

His grin widened. "I think it's amazeballs, babe."

I laughed hard and so did he. The light in his eyes flashed with heat before he bent down and kissed me.

We broke apart when all of the sudden my body was shoved to the ground and Will's weight was heavy on top of me. "Everyone, get inside," he yelled. His eyes darted around while his large frame still covered me. He panted, smelled the air, and picked me up. He quickly carried me into the house and handed me to Alder but searched my eyes. "Are you alright, Willa?"

I only nodded.

"I'll be back. Lock the door. Don't follow me," he ordered everyone.

Harris flipped the bolt. I ran to the window and watched Will stalk around the yard before disappearing around the corner of the house.

"What the fuck?" I asked.

David spoke up. "He must have heard or sensed something we didn't."

I balked. "You're vampires. How did he catch something you didn't?"

"Will is highly trained. He's been my body guard since I was turned. His father is my partner Ian's body guard. He's bloody good at what he does," David explained.

I was still skeptical, and the vampires knew it.

Harris stepped forward. "Look, everyone's okay. Let's settle down and have a drink."

I sighed, thinking about Will. He was still out there with who knows what while the vampires moved on like nothing had happened. I leaned on the kitchen island next to Trace. Micah poured a large glass of Stella Rosa Blueberry wine and Trace slid it in front of me.

"It will be okay," she assured me. "So, Esplanade..."

I perked up. "Yes. I want to do this, if you really are at a place where you want to sell Mimi's house."

Trace smiled with tears in her eyes. "I'm ready. It's time."

We hugged again and I winced just as Alder let Will back into the house. They mumbled words I couldn't hear, and Trace lifted up my shirt. A large bruise was forming over my left ribs from the fall earlier.

"Ouch, Willa. We need to get some ice on that."

Will ran to me. "Oh shit. I did that. Willa, I would never hurt you. You have to know that." His eyes pleaded for forgiveness, and he took the ice pack from Trace and pressed it to my side. I sucked in a breath. David dismissed Will and led me to the sofa. He held the ice and soothingly rubbed my knee. Will looked hurt with regret that he wasn't more careful. Micah sat on my other side and David asked Will to go to the kitchen so they could speak alone.

Great. Another threat. I was fucking sick of threats. I guess it was really time to move everyone into the same place for good. Ramp up security. Maybe add a drawbridge and build a damn moat.

Micah chuckled at my thoughts, and I stuck out my tongue at him. He ran a hand over my hair and massaged the base of my skull. My head tilted back into his palm. He cradled it and put his mouth to my ear.

"I want to taste you so bad right now."

"Just do it." I closed my eyes; his fangs sank in, and I went into another headspace. He drank my blood and the tension faded away. Micah licked the wound when he was done. We glanced around and noticed the others had left us alone. Micah hugged me and I held on tight. "Thank you. You are so good for me."

He pulled back. "I've come close to being ended twice and I'd do it all again for you."

Alder came in and kneeled in front of me. He removed the ice pack. "Your skin needs a break from the cold." He held my hand and it glowed. I sent energy into his palm. "All of the chaos and you're the one calming me, my darling."

"So, what's the situation? Do David and Will know what's going on?" Micah asked.

Alder furrowed his brow, choosing his words carefully. He rubbed his thumb over my knuckles. I sensed he was only going to give me limited information, but why?

"I didn't ask how he knows, but Will thinks one of Ian's former body guards is in town. He's bad news. He served a decade locked inside Castle Blair for plotting against Ian, the primus at the time. Someone from the inside helped him escape."

"He served a little time?" I would have thought vampires would be harsher. "Doesn't that seem like a slap on the wrist?"

Alder winced. "Castle Blair is not somewhere you want to spend even one second. People are broken there. Mind, body, and spirit."

"So, can Will handle this?" Micah asked.

"Surely," I added. "We're not talking about a vengeful vampire or ego crazed witch."

Alder nodded and squeezed my hand. "The clutch will increase security. I may ask you and Trace to do a few protection spells."

"Of course. Marita hooking us up with the local coven has been helpful. There is so much Trace and I have learned in a short time."

"I love seeing you embracing your roots," Alder said then he kissed my forehead. He noticed the fading wound on my neck where Micah took a taste. It was almost gone. Alder ran a hand through Micah's hair and pulled his mouth up to meet his lips. Alder's tongue brushed Micah's and they both grunted.

"And thank you for just being you," he said to Micah. "You complete us and are always what Willa needs. You two are so in tune. That alone is magical."

I sat there swooning as David and Will walked into the room followed by Harris and Trace. Will swayed for a second, then smiled. "It's buzzing in here."

David pointed at me. "That's Willa."

"Oh, yes. I was lucky enough to feel her energy the first night we met when I drove her to your runway show," he said wistfully. He and David sat on the matching sofa opposite ours.

Will's demeanor became serious. "While I can't tell you exactly why Rafe is coming around, I'm not ruling out anything. Maybe he has it out for David now that he's the primus of the London clutch. He may have heard about everything that went down with Wesley and the coven and now he wants your magic. As shift—" Will corrected himself, "um, body guards we're taught not to trust witches fully. There's always been a separation of cultures between vampires and witches. Going back further than my father's generation, we learned to keep away if we can. Witches can be powerful enemies. And we, as well as vampires, peacefully live with limited contact."

"I guess that all changed when Harris and I found Willa and Trace," Alder said.

"Yes, and I never thought I would ever be near a witch, but now I can't seem to stay away," David smoldered. "If Rafe is after me, and I put any of you in danger..."

I spoke up. "Then we will deal with it. How big of a threat can one human be against vampires and witches?"

Will furrowed his brow and thought about his next words. "He's cunning, but I'm sure you're right. David, you should call Ian. I'll talk to Dad. Tell them to stay alert. Maybe you and Willa should check out of the hotel. Stay close to the safety of your own here with us."

David sighed. "Yeah, I guess you're right."

"Wish we had the keys to the Esplanade property now. We need the room," Trace said.

Alder jumped up and took out his phone. "Let me see what I can do. We want the place for sure, right?"

We all answered with a collective yes.

DAVID

Alder secured the new place with no issues and after resting the next day, we were up as soon as the sun set to pack Willa and Trace's necessities. Alder graciously deeded me one of the apartments with an extra room. This would allow Willa to have her own area for decompressing within my space when needed, plus an extra room if Will accompanied me on my trips here. I assumed he would, but that was before. Before he and Willa had a moment. Before Willa used the word bond.

The property had been deep cleaned for showings, so there was only a small amount of dust to take care of. So far, I only had a dresser, the bed Will was using at the other place, and a sofa that had been in Trace's attic. I unpacked my things and heard a vacuum running. Will vigorously ran the nozzle over the cushions and between every crevice of what would be his bed until we secured more furnishings. I handed him a quilt.

"Thanks, boss. I think I'll go for a run. Get a look around the neighborhood."

"Alone? You'll be okay?"

"Sure thing. I'm faster than Rafe should he turn up. I kinda wish he would. I wouldn't be opposed to a good fight."

"Be careful, mate. If you're gone too long, the vampire search party will come looking for you."

Willa brought a few towels and put them in the en suite. There was a knock on the door less than two minutes after Will left and Trace peeked in. "Harris and I are taking a break. Coffee and Vena in about ten."

"Brilliant, thanks."

I pulled Willa against my chest and kissed her. She pulled back and searched my eyes. "I'm sorry we won't be alone for a couple of nights."

My hands squeezed her hips. "I'm a vampire, babe. I have all the time in the world. Keeping our family safe comes before anything else."

Willa smiled. "Our family." She kissed me, still smiling. "Yes, our family."

We found everyone at the long bar of what would soon be the first vampire coffee shop. Trace sorted bundles of sage and abalone shells. Then, lit lavender incense and placed them in holders to be put in each apartment as well as the shop.

"We're going to do this right. We'll smudge after the incense burns down," she instructed. "Willa and I will show you all how to cleanse every corner."

A barely audible noise caught my attention, and I went to the door of the shop to find Marita about to knock. I opened the door and surprised her with a hug.

"Oh, well, hello, David," she laughed.

Trace and Willa made a high-pitched squeal in unison when they saw her.

"You guys! You picked the perfect location for tarot. There are a few others nearby, but during certain seasons, they are booked up so far in advance. Everyone knows to come to Marigny for a reading. And Trace is legit," Marita said.

"Did they tell you we are opening a vampire coffee shop?" Alder asked.

Marita's jaw dropped. "No, they most certainly did not."

Willa winced. "You don't think the other witches will be mad, do you? I mean, witches and vampires mingling together?"

"Well, we are planning on closing the shop to humans at 1

a.m.," Trace added. "We're going to spread the word so that most vampires won't even show up until after."

Marita smiled. "I think it may be a good thing to bring us together. We couldn't have saved Willa and Micah without each other."

"Truth." Micah raised his glass of Vena then took a swig.

"So, have you named the place yet?" Marita asked.

"I'm sure Willa and Trace will come up with something brilliant and sexy," I said.

Willa gave me a hip bump. "You know it."

Harris emptied his glass. "Alright, while the witches smudge, the vampires will secure the windows with blackout shades and shutters. Grab a drill, mates."

WILL

Damn, I loved a good long run. Even if I wasn't a shifter, I think I would still feel the primal need to be out in the night air smelling leaves, pavement, and other creatures of the night. Good thing I love it. Protecting vampires is a dusk till dawn job. It's hard to imagine anything or anyone having better senses than vampires, but we do. In a crowd, sounds and smells find us first.

I had to get out of the house. Seeing David and Willa together made my cock hard and a wave of possessiveness crashed over me that I couldn't explain. I didn't know what the future held, but I knew in my marrow that she was mine. Or maybe I was hers. Maybe I had it all wrong but fighting it the short time I had been in New Orleans became almost unbearable. I wouldn't be able to fight it for much longer. When shifters fall, they fall hard. Everyone uses the word bond like they know what it means. To bond with a shifter isn't a little welding between iron that could snap with enough force. The only thing that could break a bond was death. Sure, a shifter may not end up with their mate, but the bond remained. If Willa was my mate and she or her vampires rejected me, I would live an unfulfilled life. Never satisfied with anyone else. As far as I knew, a shifter had never bonded with a witch and if the said witch had three vampire mates, what the fuck was I going to do? It was unprecedented, but it seemed the world I knew was changing. I had always been intrigued with tarot and I couldn't wait to see what Trace's cards might reveal.

I had been so deep inside my own mind I hadn't been paying attention to my surroundings much. Just paws on asphalt. When a car or human came, I leapt over the nearest hedge or fence and continued running out of sight. It wouldn't be good to be seen. There were no wolves in Louisiana, or London for that matter, but we had our safe places there. I would have to learn them here. I figured it was best to stay out of the French Quarter. Humans partied or roamed all night long there. Yes, the perimeter of Marigny seemed to be a bit quieter.

I came back around to the place I started. I had left my clothes and a bottle of water hidden behind the chapel in Saint Roch Cemetery. I love cemeteries. They were great places to be left alone and not be seen. I thought about Willa. What would it be like to bring her here and walk hand in hand, reading names on tombstones? Stealing a kiss? My heart hurt a little at the thought, but I would take the fantasy of having her even if I couldn't in real life. I had fantasized about her plenty. Every night since I had picked her up outside David's flat in London. And feeling the energy that flowed from her hand gave me a high like never before. It was difficult handing her off that night and harder staying away when her troublemaking brother showed up, but I was around. I had been there with my father, patrolling the alley behind the building Willa and Micah were held in. We kept out of sight but were there if we were needed. I would have killed for David, but if Willa had been hurt by Wesley, he would have been ended slowly and painfully. And vampires would last a very *very* long time before they begged for an ending to their agony. My father took me to Blair Castle once. I witnessed firsthand how terribly tortuous the place was.

As if my thoughts of the castle had conjured him up, I smelled Rafe. He was close and he wasn't alone. Fuck. I was in the mood for a fight, but taking two wolves on at once did not give me a favorable outcome. I should have known Rafe wouldn't have come alone. One shifter is no match against a vampire, and Willa had four on her side, maybe more.

I quickly shifted back to wolf and my ears perked up. My nostrils flared at a familiar smell. My fucking brother. Levi was older and a wee bit bigger than me, and I was big, and his hatred for me ran deep. He was in line to be the protector of the primus, but I got the job. His younger, *adopted* brother stole the position that should've been his. The problem with Levi was he couldn't put down the bottle. A body guard sloshed on whiskey was no good to anyone. None of the vampires trusted him with their lives, so he mainly took jobs as a bouncer at various bars and clubs. But those never lasted long either because of the easy access to booze. Hell, Rafe had probably bribed him with his favorite drink.

They were getting closer, and I couldn't run back to Esplanade. There was no way I could lead them to everyone else. I wasn't sure how long I had been out, and I didn't have time to shift back to human to retrieve my cell and send a 9-1-1 text to David. I would have to do my best on my own.

Surprisingly, Rafe and Levi were in their human forms, walking through the graveyard like they were on a casual stroll. Levi had a shit eating grin on his face. I snarled a little as a warning. They stopped, keeping a good distance between us.

"Shift and get your fucking clothes on, brother," Levi barked. They knew I didn't trust them when I held my ground.

Rafe moved one step backwards. "We just want to talk, mate."

Shifters can't communicate telepathically, so I reluctantly complied. My eyes never left the pair while I dressed. "Why did you come here?"

Levi pulled a flask from his waistband and took a drink then offered it to me.

"Fuck off, Levi. You're pissed and I'm not in the mood." I turned my attention to Rafe. "Why him? You can do better."

I knew this would incense Levi. Rafe was the lowest company one could keep. Levi's shoulders heaved with anger, and he spit when he shouted. "Bastard!"

He lunged at me, but Rafe grabbed his shoulder. "No! We're not killing him...tonight. You're miffed that he's telling the truth. Rafe the wretch. Isn't that what they call me? But no. Neither one of us can do better."

Levi paced in a small circle while looking up to the stars, trying to cool his temper. All the while growling in a low tone.

"Oh, you know it's true," he said to Levi.

"Are you two done with your lover's quarrel, I'm beat."

Their eyes flared at me. I succeeded in insulting them both. "Get on with it."

Rafe spoke calmly. "Are your vampires back in London without you? No one's at the house. Did they leave you here as a distraction?"

So, Rafe and Levi weren't aware we had relocated. That was good. My racing heart slowed down. "You're not going to get any information from me. You should know that. My boss has powerful friends. You won't get to him. I'm even cautious around the bloody witches."

I had to make them think I wanted nothing to do with the witches. Keeping Willa off of their radar was high priority.

"Have you not heard about her magic, mate," Rafe asked excitedly. He looked as if he got off just thinking about it. How dare he think about Willa. My heart sped up again and the urge to shift rumbled within, but I had to remain indifferent.

"Rubbish. It's only energy play. Nothing more. She's no more magical than my bollocks."

"If you say so," Rafe replied. "Go off now. We have to sleep. Keep a look over your shoulder. We'll be around." And with that they took off north, which was the opposite way I needed to go. I sighed with relief and texted David.

Hey, boss. Headed back now.

He was waiting on the porch when I returned.

DAVID

Will looked sweaty and tired. I knew from the look on his face that something had happened.

"You haven't smelled them around here, have you?" Will asked.

"Not since I came outside. Why don't we go in? We can talk while you shower."

We walked around the front through the courtyard to our flat. Will undressed while I sat on the toilet, and I couldn't help but notice how beautiful he was. It's like I saw him for the first time even though he had been my protector since I had turned. He moaned as the hot water ran over his body and my mind wandered, watching him through the glass door. I imagined myself joining him, and then I fantasized about Willa in between. My trousers grew tight, and I looked away and scolded myself for the torrid thoughts.

"My brother is here. With Rafe. They tracked me to Saint Roche Cemetery."

"Oh, shit." This wasn't good for Will. We could easily defend ourselves together, but this meant that Will couldn't be alone.

"I know. He is still a wanker most of the time, I think. He may not be much help for whatever Rafe has in mind. They don't know the lot of us have relocated yet. I hope to keep it that way as long as possible."

"You better stay closer the next time you venture out. I've been to Saint Roch. It's a bit too far for comfort," I said as Will turned off the water. I handed him a towel and he grinned.

"You worried about me, boss?"

Damnit, I blushed. I felt the heat on my cheeks. "Well, I do care." That's all I said. But I felt much more. Will had become a part of me. My right-hand man, protector, friend...and the sparks of a new physical attraction couldn't be denied.

The door opened without a knock and Willa froze in place. She looked at me then stared at Will standing in a towel. Her mouth hung open.

"Uhhh," Willa stammered.

"Hello, Willa," Will practically purred with a sexy smile.

I took her hand. "Come on, babe. It's almost time to rest. Goodnight, Will."

"Night, boss. Sleep well, Willa."

I pulled her into the bedroom, and she still looked startled.

"Are you alright?" I asked her.

Willa sat on the foot of the bed. "Oh, peachy keen," she said sarcastically. "I didn't mean to barge in. I'll have to be more careful. I don't want to see Will half naked again."

I laughed. "Does that bother you?"

She scoffed. "Yes. I don't even know him. Not really. I don't know. Now I'm annoyed and I don't even know why." She sighed.

I knew why. She was fighting it. Fighting the feelings that he stirred within. The internal struggle of not wanting Will was written all over her face. She picked at the skin around her fingernails, so I grabbed her hands and threw them over her head, pushing her back onto the mattress. I held her wrists down with one hand while the other cupped a breast and squeezed.

"Oh, David," she moaned.

I kissed the thoughts right out of her pretty head and made her mind and body forget all about Will. Willa was usually the dominant one in our relationship, but I knew what she needed physically in the moment. Calming the storm of her emotions was an act of my obedience. I devotedly surrendered all authority to my liege.

Seven

WILLA

I slid out of David's bed while the sun was still in the sky. Trace and I wanted to go to Marita's for some witchy provisions and then arrange Trace's tarot parlor. The coffee shop would take longer to set up, but Trace already had a long list of clients wanting a reading in person.

I tiptoed behind the sofa where Will lay sleeping. I stopped to look at him. My hand itched to sweep the dark curls that hung over his eyes to the side. I don't know what got into me, but I did it. Slowly. His hair was silky between my fingertips. I ran one finger over his eyebrow. He groaned at my touch and started to roll over but suddenly sat up when he felt my presence and quickly grabbed one of my wrists.

I gasped. We stared at each other. He didn't say anything. I wished he would. Energy throbbed down my arm and vibrated against his palm. Will pulled me around the couch and down to sit beside him. He let go and brushed a lock of hair behind my ear.

"Willa."

Our eyes remained locked. I think we were both afraid to say what we were thinking, so I tried my best to lift the heavy air of want between us.

"I'm sorry. I didn't mean to wake you. Trace and I are going to the boutique. You go back to sleep."

I stood, but he grabbed my hand. "Wait. Let me go with you."

I shook my head. "No. no. We're fine. You rest."

He stood up and thankfully had on boxer briefs. He folded the quilt. "The boss would kill me if anything happened to you. He's good and we will be back before the sun sets, right?"

"Umm, yes. I guess you can come."

Will bolted to the bathroom. "Give me five minutes."

I found Trace lounging on a chair beside the empty pool, reading a book.

"Good afternoon, bestie." She beamed.

"You love this place, don't you? It *is* perfect."

Trace closed the book. "The vibes are peaceful, but also exciting and fresh and new."

"I agree. Oh, Will is coming with."

I hadn't told her about what was going on between us. I didn't know how. He walked across the courtyard looking hot as hell. His jeans fit just right and his thin navy blue sweater accentuated perfectly toned arms.

"Ladies." He tilted his head to greet us, then leaned down and kissed Trace's cheek then mine. I heard his nose take in my scent before he stood back up.

"Hi, Will." Trace smiled cheerfully.

I drove my Jeep and Will sat in the backseat singing to the music the entire way. Trace and I laughed, but he was surprisingly good. It only made him more endearing, and I was impressed he knew the lyrics to the songs of my favorite band, Missio. I really needed him to not be so likable. I made up my mind. I would try my best to block his energy. He was David's body guard, and I didn't think that would be changing any time soon. We would often be in close proximity, so we could be friends, but that's all. At least, that's what I told myself.

"Long time no see," Marita joked when she hugged me and Trace. "And I haven't had the pleasure..." She held out her hand.

Will took it. "Marita, I'm Will. I've heard a lot about you."

"Oh, really? Because I haven't heard anything about you."

He smiled but looked uncomfortable. "Well, I work for David Kingswood."

Marita's eyes narrowed. "A protector."

Will's eyes darted around. "Erm...I've been his *body guard* since he became the most famous model in London."

Marita nodded then smiled again. "I see. Well, it's nice to meet you."

The entire exchange seemed odd. The energy in the shop felt off to me. I would have to talk to Marita later. She read people so well. Maybe she sensed negativity in Will, and I trusted her judgement. Trace meandered around as if she hadn't noticed, filling the tote she brought with candles and spices.

Will touched my elbow. "I think I'll step outside. The incense is a bit strong for my nose. I'll be right outside the door."

I nodded and he went out. I rolled my eyes at Marita while Trace emptied her things onto the counter.

"I desperately need to get the parlor open ASAP to fund my habit. My clients are ready. You know, I was doing readings online. It's so sweet some of them are excited to meet me. It makes me feel good about what I do."

Marita looked at us both. "You are just beginning in your journey. I think you two have more power than you know."

I glanced at the door. "What do you think about Will? Get any first impressions?"

Marita smiled. "He's gorgeous."

I rolled my eyes again. "You know what I mean!"

She got serious. "I think he must be brave and trustworthy and good at what he does to be working for David." Then she leaned in and touched my hand. "Is there something between the two of you?"

My jaw dropped. Trace's eyes went wide.

"Willa! What?"

I shook my head. "No. No no no." I tried to play it off. "That's crazy. What would I do with another man. I'm allllll manned up."

"When we shook hands, his thoughts were of you," Marita revealed.

I stammered for a second. "It's probably because he's looking out for me. Uh, me *and* Trace while we are out. He said David would kill him if anything happened. I'm sure that's all it is."

"Whatever you say," Trace teased.

I quickly changed the subject. "You'll have to come by again. We're setting up the parlor tonight."

"Of course, and I'm bringing a housewarming gift." She winked.

When we got back to Esplanade the sun hid behind the skyline and the whole house was alive. A moving truck sat in front, the vampires were up, and quite a few I recognized from the clutch were carrying furniture inside. Harris came out onto the porch and waved.

"Oh, my stuff is here," Trace exclaimed.

She ran into Harris' arms with a kiss. He squeezed her tight. Will took her tote from the Jeep since she completely forgot about her purchases. He placed his hand on the small of my back and I made sure none of my energy made it to his fingertips. I tried to be as resistible as possible. But if I was honest with myself, his touch soothed me. It felt normal and that scared me.

Alder's lips met mine as soon as I walked through the front door. Then Micah held me in a hug from behind. "Here we go being a whoreo again," I joked.

We parted and then I heard a beautiful sound. All of the chatter and noise around me faded away. I followed the sensuous flow of musical notes to David who sat at a black baby grand piano beside the staircase, running his long fingers over the keys. Each note, smooth and connected, pulled me to him like he was the shining silver moon, and I was the obedient ocean tide. I stood there enthralled. I was unaware he had the same effect on the others. They were all watching as well.

He glanced over his shoulder and met my eyes with a smolder, and I went nearer. Seeing him touch the keys made me want to touch him and I let my fingers stroke the short black curls on the back of his neck. David gave a satisfied groan as he played the final sad notes. Everyone clapped as he wound an arm around my waist. I kissed the top of his head. "Thank you for playing. I loved it."

Will came over, but he didn't look at me. His eyes were on David. The look on his face was more than that of a body guard or even a friend. It was the look of love.

Eight

DAVID

I began playing as soon as I knew Willa had walked in. I played for her. There was no need to thank me. I was thankful every second I got to spend in her presence.

When I turned around Will was close. The look in his glittering brown eyes gave me a little jolt. He surprised me. I kept my arm around Willa but reached to squeeze his hand. I wanted him to know that I noticed. "That one was beautiful, boss." He gave a meek smile and attempted to shake off the attraction still swirling between us. Will had heard me play in the past, but we hadn't experienced this undeniable thread being woven from his being to mine before.

Willa leaned in front of me. "You must be hungry, Will. We should order delivery. I'm hungry too."

Her tone seemed a bit like a mum to a child. Was she being overly nice, condescending, or bitchy? I genuinely couldn't tell. Willa held me closer. Was she *jealous*?

I chimed in. "See what everyone wants." I took out my credit card and handed it to Will. "We'll be right back," I stated as I pulled Willa out of the shop to the far side of the courtyard.

"What was that, babe?"

"What?" Her chin tilted up in defiance.

"With Will. You're jealous."

She scoffed. "Jealous? Of whom? Will? And you?"

My eyebrows furrowed together. She damn well was something. "Who else? You talked down to him in there. Why?"

Willa huffed and sighed and looked very irritated. She growled and fisted her hands at her sides.

"I'm annoyed, alright. I'm just...I don't know. I hate not understanding the vibes I'm getting from him. I hate having to block his energy and having to hold back mine. He's your body guard. He's not going anywhere. I have to deal with all of this, and I hate *thinking* about him."

I grabbed her arms. They pulsed with waves of frustration. I made her look at me. "Why are you holding back your energy?"

Her shoulders relaxed and her eyes went soft.

"Because I'm falling for him and if he feels that, then there's no going back."

A tear ran down her cheek. I'd be lying if I said my heart didn't feel like it twisted in my chest. I already knew this would happen as soon as she mentioned the bond. I knew, if it was real, it couldn't be undone. But Willa was fighting it, and I didn't blame her. She didn't choose this. Her mates had no say. The universe had thrown a curve ball at her. At all of us. She didn't yet know the whole truth about Will. Would it cause her to spiral? Would Will hate me if I told her? I kept my mouth shut and pulled her against my chest.

WILLA

Neither one of us said anything else. I was tired of thinking about it and David probably didn't know what to think. He came all the way to New Orleans to spend time with me. This was not the way I had imagined it would be. I looped my arm through his and we went back inside.

"Pizza will be here in ten," Will casually mentioned like I hadn't been a total bitch before.

I smiled faintly. "Oh, perfect."

"Alder ordered one loaded with black olives just for you," Micah poked at me.

45

My stomach rumbled. "I might share if you ask nicely," I teased him. He feigned a shocked look and grabbed me up, twirling me off of my feet. He didn't put me down, so I squirmed and laughed. "What are you doing?"

"We've got about five minutes, right? We'll be back," Micah stated to everyone as he carried me to the bathroom. He closed the door with his foot and sat me on the counter, next to the faucet. He sweetly tucked my hair behind my ears.

"You were crying."

I held his palm to my cheek and kissed it. He leaned down and his lips met mine with a contented hum. I slipped my tongue into his mouth and let the confusion I had been feeling filter out of my mind. We made out until we heard Alder knock twice.

"Better come get your pizza before Will eats it all," he warned through the door.

Micah and I giggled, and I kissed the end of his nose. "You're so good for me. Have I ever told you that?"

"Don't ever forget it."

WILL

Willa was avoiding me like the plague. She wouldn't even look at me. I devoured an extra-large pizza and decided to go out for a while. And I would pay attention to the neighborhood this time. Get a lay of the land and, if I was honest, get a good shag. I had confidence I would find a willing woman. Shifters give off irresistible pheromones. It had been weeks since I'd pulled a tidy one and being around Willa and her mates made my cock rock hard twenty-four-seven.

"Hey, boss. Mind if I head out for the night?"

David knew exactly what I meant and nodded in approval. I met Marita on the porch on the way out.

"Nice to see you again, Will."

She shook my hand and held on. I was frozen for a minute. When she let go, I shook it off, but she still held my attention.

"There is turmoil inside. Inside you and those close to you. What is meant to be will be. You will want to bury down what you know is true. You'll want to run away from it but take this head on and you will come out on the other side better for it."

I didn't know how to respond, so I turned to go.

"Hey, Will, be patient with her."

I nodded and left.

Bloody witches and their magic. My world was changing, and I'd better get on board. I had to stop myself from obsessing over what Marita said. My chest heaved as I took heavy breaths. Music from a nearby club drew me down the sidewalk. A fit blonde in a tight black dress stood outside, smoking. Clove cigarettes. I had always loved the smell. She looked like she worked in the place. A waitress maybe.

I smiled at her and went inside. I sat on one of the two open stools at the bar. It was a busy place, not much different than the pubs in London. I ordered a gin and tonic and spun around to watch the locals. Plenty of beautiful women caught my eye, but the girl from outside came in and joined a group that was there for a bachelorette party. She looked my way several times before actually coming over.

"Are you from around here?" she asked in a southern American accent.

I chuckled. "No, lass. And you?"

Her eyes lit up. "Oh, you're British. Like Harry Styles. I love it." She gestured to her friends. "We came down from Nashville. My sister's getting hitched tomorrow."

"Smashing. I'll buy a round. What's her favorite?"

She licked her lips. "Well, *I* could use a screaming orgasm right about now."

The zipper of my jeans became painfully pressed on my cock. My eyes held hers and when my jaw flexed, she grabbed my arm and pulled me into the bathroom. I glanced around to see it was fairly clean, so my hands jerked up the tiny skirt to grab her ass while she kissed my neck. No panties. She was small and I didn't want to kneel down on the questionable floor, so I lifted her up against the wall and went down on her. If she wanted a screaming orgasm, that's what I'd give her. With pleasure. She panted, trying to be quiet, then tugged my hair hard when she came. I put her on her feet and her knees were weak. I kissed her clove flavored lips, letting her taste her own cum as her hands freed my cock.

"It's not going to take long," I confessed, quickly stretching a condom over my bellend. She gasped with the first thrust.

"I don't give a shit. Fuck me."

We ordered shots and took them to the table of woozy women. They cheered and looked at me like I was the only gent in the place.

I leaned into the blonde's ear, "What's your name?"

"Oh, shit. It's Maggie." She spouted a list of everyone at the table like I would remember their names.

"I'm Will."

"Hi, Willlll," they said in unison.

Damn, these Tennessee girls knew how to have a good time and were *very* friendly. I kissed every one of them at some point in the night except the bride to be. I did have some self-respect and respect for her future groom. Plus, she was Maggie's sister. Couldn't go there.

Maggie clung to me outside while I said my goodbyes. "I don't have a date to the wedding."

I peeled her away. "I can't, darling."

She pouted, "Come on. I'll give you a blowy in the back of the opera house before I do my bridesmaid walk."

Shit. Tempting...I got hard again.

I sighed. "I really can't. Believe me I so would."

Maggie slipped her number into the front pocket of my jeans and felt the form of my dick while she was there. She stroked it a few times to torment me.

"Mmm. Call me if you change your mind."

I made sure the group left safely in their Ubers before heading back.

Willa, Trace, and Marita were admiring their work in the parlor. There were more members of the Hunt clutch I had never met milling around, talking about how great the shop looked.

I exited through the courtyard and found David in his place. He sat on the couch busy on his laptop.

"Hey, boss."

He looked up with raised eyebrows. "Oh, have a look at your room."

It had been furnished. Everything fresh and new and in sleek black. My clothes were folded in stacks on one side of the bed. David stood in the doorway with a grin.

"Come in. This is brill. Thanks, boss."

David sat on the edge of my new bed, and I undressed. I sniffed the jumper and wrinkled my nose. "Bloody smoke."

"Did you have it off?"

I sighed wistfully. "Ahh, yeah. Chatted up sweet Maggie."

He laughed. "Maggie?"

"A tidy lass from Tennessee. I hate that we shagged standing up in the loo, but my knob was full of beans, know what I mean? My arse needs to be in the gym. I don't have a body fit for eternity like yours."

"You're built like a tower, mate. I'll find you a good gym for when we are here. You don't need that much work, you know."

I glanced at David's face. He stared. It was almost uncomfortable, but there was a strange attraction between us again. I stepped closer and leaned over.

"Do I smell like a pub?"

David stuck his nose in my brown curls. He took in my scent. "You bloody do, mate."

I stood back up. He huffed and laid back on the comforter. "Grab a shower. You're giving off loads of pheromones."

His feet were still on the floor. I boldly stepped in between his knees and saw his hard on through his trousers.

"Hey, boss?"

He sighed again, staring at the ceiling. "Yes?"

I jumped back when Willa walked in. I couldn't believe I hadn't heard or smelled her.

"Heyyy." I looked down, remembering I was naked, and quickly covered my cock. Blimey, this looked bad. "Sorry, Willa. I... wow, this is embarrassing."

David had sat up. "Hey, Babe. Will has a wee little problem with his..." He gestured to my undercarriage.

I recovered. "I have a lump...in my sack and I can't see it."

She looked genuinely concerned. "Well, is it okay?" she asked David.

"Yeah. I think so. Feels kind of like a cyst, but he's going to get it checked out by a professional."

"I'm gonna get a shower. Oh, thanks for my new room." I grabbed a pair of sweats from the top of the stack, gave David a relieved look, and ducked into the lavatory.

Nine

WILLA

After waking up the next evening, I climbed on top of David and laid on his chest. His arms held me tight.

"We should probably get out of bed," he said sleepily.

I wiggled against him. "Or we could...go to your office and break in your new desk."

He was up and carrying me before I could utter another word. Will was sitting at the little island in the kitchen, eating. He had white powdered sugar stuck to his five o'clock shadow.

"I went out and got beignets. Fresh hot chocolate too."

David kept walking. "We'll be right back."

"Thank you," I offered as David shut his office door with one foot. He fucked me fast and hard, and it was just what I needed. What we both needed after the whirlwind of the past few days.

I figured Will wouldn't look at us when we returned. He had to hear, but his eyes were on me. I sat across from him and he slid a large cup of hot cocoa in front of me.

"Thanks again," I said quietly. It was becoming a struggle, not knowing how to interact with him. He smiled.

"I can't believe I hadn't made it to Café Du Monde before now. I bought loads." He laughed.

David stood over the sink, letting the sugar fall away from his bare chest. "Mmm. I do still love real food," he mumbled with a mouthful.

"I mean, you'd have to be a monster to not enjoy beignets," I said, licking my fingertips.

We all laughed together, and it felt comfortable. I was thankful. David gave me an endearing look.

"I think I'll go visit Alder and Micah for a little while. Grab a shower before the business consultant arrives. I'm excited to get everything planned out."

I hopped off my chair and kissed David's lips. "See you, babe," he whispered.

It was quiet when I entered our place. I put an ear to the bedroom door and heard Micah moaning. I smiled and wanted to see my mates together, pleasuring one another, so I slipped inside the room. Micah met my gaze while Alder continued swirling his tongue around Micah's cock. Micah bit his lip and gasped. I ran my hand up through Alder's dark hair and he kept going.

"Don't stop. Meet me in the shower when you're done." I couldn't help myself from getting off before they joined me.

Much to my surprise, the business consultant Alder hired was Thomas. Trace and I were delighted we would be working with someone we knew and trusted. He had moved on from Leona with grace and looked so healthy and vibrant, the way a vampire should look, without her.

"My friends." He hugged us. "I can't tell you how thrilled I am to be here. Your idea of a vampire coffee shop is brilliant. I wish I would have thought of it myself," he said with a wink.

Thomas had a solid business plan and had been in contact with the coffee company side of Vena. They were sold on the idea and had sent their own pitch for Thomas to present. There were various tea blends. Bloody Good Coffee for true vampires, traditional and decaf for humans. He showed us a contract and explained every line.

"They have another idea I think is smart. Whatever you name the place would incorporate the name of the main coffee blend. Do you have one you fancy?"

Trace spoke up. "I wrote down at least twenty, but I have a favorite. After Dark Coffee Shop and Tarot Parlor."

I grinned. "I love it. After Dark. So perfect."

Alder nodded. "Yes. I love it too. It's not overtly obvious. It's subtle and classy."

Thomas flipped pages in the pitch document. "So, the blends for humans would be called After Dark and After Dark Decaf. And we're keeping Bloody Good for us vamps." He jotted them down in the blanks. "I will take this to them and get back with you. Shouldn't take long. They'll love it. I'm sure of it. I know I'll be a regular."

We walked Thomas out and saw Will, dressed in sweats, leaving through the courtyard. He waved.

"Going for a run?" I asked.

He pivoted and came to the porch. Trace and Alder went back inside, leaving us alone. Will stared at me. He was human and didn't have the vampire light in his eyes but had his own smoldering look that held my gaze and I felt sparks between us. We stood there for a long while. I sighed, trying not to reach out and touch him. It seemed like I always wanted to touch his brown curls lately. He shifted back and forth on his feet. The trance his gaze held me in broke and I tore my eyes away.

"I should let you go. You were about to go out."

He shook his head and smiled. "Oh. Yeah. I was. I mean, I am. Shit, I didn't mean to keep you out here."

"No, I...it's okay." I felt so awkward all of the sudden. I really needed to figure out how to act around him.

He sniffed the air and glanced around. "I have to go. You know, so I can be back before sunrise." He turned to leave.

"Hey, Will."

He looked at me again. "Yeah?"

"Be careful."

He smiled again and winked before jogging down the sidewalk. I watched until he disappeared around the corner, and I went back inside.

WILL

I caught the scent of Rafe too close for comfort. I had to distance myself from Esplanade.

Rafe was definitely an alpha. His scent masked the smell of my brother, but I was sure they were running together. Levi wouldn't do well alone in a city he wasn't used to. Too bad for Rafe he was the alpha of nothing and no one. As far as I knew, he hadn't bonded with anyone. That alone makes a shifter bitter, but factor in the time spent in Castle Blair and the anger and spite would build like the perfect storm. I was aware of how volatile Rafe and Levi could be together.

The bond between Willa and me was now undeniable. It grew deeper every time our eyes met. It made me feel stronger as a shifter. Like I could take on the world. I didn't know what all of this meant yet or what the future held. David had become Willa's mate. I was his protector, but now bonded to her. It was unprecedented, so the rules I had lived by before had to change. I guessed. Hell, I had no idea.

I ran to the Marigny Opera House as a human. I didn't see anyone around, so I went around back to the secluded area next to the air conditioning units and dropped my clothes. After shifting, I waited. I smelled Rafe again. I waited, listening, but growing anxious. I heard a low growl and raised my hackles. I leapt over a hedge from my position, so I wouldn't be in such a tight space. Backed into a corner wasn't where I wanted to be.

A snarl from the shadows near the back door of the opera house caught my attention. Rafe. If I could attack while he was in the small space of the alcove, I might have a leg up. I took my opportunity and jumped, latching onto the thick fur along his spine. He yelped, but before I could get to the sweet spot, his throat, I felt claws digging deep into my shoulders. Levi had waited in the open doorway, hidden. His claws were hooked into my hide, and he dragged me, scratching at the floor, into the opera house where no one would see the scene. I thrashed about and Levi's claws released my skin but ripped open my flesh. I had never been in so much pain. I slashed at him with my paw and caught him across the neck. It stunned him and he choked. Rafe howled and knocked me against a wall. The back of my head hit hard, and Rafe bit down on my throat. His jaws locked and fangs penetrated fur, skin, fat, and muscle. I knew he wouldn't let go. There was no oxygen getting to my lungs. I went limp in his mouth, and he dropped my body into a growing pool of blood. I heard Rafe howl before the building went silent.

WILL

How could I have let it happen? I was smarter than that. It hurt to breathe. Hell, everything hurt as I slowly crawled under hedges, cars, and anything that would keep me somewhat out of sight. And there would surely be a blood trail. I had lost a lot and my legs trembled. It took me a long time to get anywhere near our house. The sun would soon rise. There just wasn't enough energy within me to shift back to human. My clothes and cell phone remained beside the opera house. I had never been so frightened or close to death. Fuck me.

Ten

WILLA

T race and I were a little tipsy from celebrating the soon to be business deal. Okay, a lot tipsy. The visiting vampires from the Hunt clutch were long gone. Trace and Harris went to their place, and I made out with Alder, Micah, and David in the king-sized bed in David's room for the last hour before sunrise. Hands and mouths delved into every pleasurable possibility.

Alder and Micah gave me very long goodbye kisses, David jumped into the shower before we would rest, and I foraged in the pantry for cookies. I needed a snack after the round of heavy petting with happy endings. I laughed to myself thinking about Will and that he would probably be hungry too. He was always hungry.

Will! I hadn't noticed him return from his run. Did he? Should I peek into his room? Yes? No? Shit, I wasn't sure what to do.

David stuck his head out of the bedroom. "You good? We should go to bed. To *sleep* this time." He winked.

I padded over to Will's door and listened.

"Did you see Will come home?"

David's eyes narrowed. "You know what? I didn't." He walked

over next to me and listened as well. Silence. He knocked a few times. Nothing.

I put my hand on the knob and got a bad feeling.

"I don't think he's in there," I whispered as tears welled up in my eyes.

David looked concerned over the emotion I showed. "Oh, babe. It's alright." He removed my hand from the knob and slowly opened the door. Will hadn't come back.

David ran to put on a shirt.

"The sun's about to come up," I yelled. "You can't go out there!"

I dashed in front of him before he reached the door to leave. I planted my palms on his chest. "Stop. You can't. I mean it. I'll go look around. I'll get Trace to help."

He remained tense but ran a hand through his hair and sighed in acceptance of the situation. I knew David felt helpless, but he too realized he couldn't risk it. "Okay, alright. The sun can't reach my bedroom. Come back to me as soon as you get any information or if anything happens. I'll be waiting. I can do without rest for a day if needed." I kissed him and assured him I would and that we would be careful.

I stepped outside into the courtyard and into the first light of morning. I stopped and glanced around. Then I noticed the blood. At first, I panicked, but then I was addled. The crimson drips and grisly smears led from the courtyard gate all the way down into the empty pool. I creeped to the ledge. What in the hell was I looking at? A very large, mortally wounded beast? I saw dark gray or black, blood matted fur in the shape of a canine that appeared deceased. Great. We didn't need this complication with all of the other shit going on. I knew I needed backup, so I ran to get Trace.

I banged on her door. Trace cracked it open. "What the hell? Why are you up? Something's wrong. What's wrong?"

She pulled me into the living room, and I pushed her to her bedroom.

"Get dressed in comfortable clothes. I need your help. I'll explain in the courtyard. Oh, bring a towel you don't mind getting blood and fur on."

Trace's eyes were wide, but she hurried. She let Harris know what was going on before the two of us headed outside. We stood, looking down at the pitiful creature. It wasn't moving.

"Looks like a wolf, but there are no wolves in New Orleans," Trace said.

"What if one escaped the Audubon Zoo? That would explain why it's hurt, being out in the wild," I whispered. "I don't know if they even have wolves. Oh, and...Will didn't come home last night. That's what I was coming to tell you, but then I found this thing."

We still stood there, unsure of what to do.

Trace pushed up the sleeves of her sweatshirt. "Well, we have to check it out. If it's dead, we can deal with it later." She tentatively went down the steps of the pool and I followed. In my heart, I hoped it was dead, so I could focus on Will being gone. Trace squatted next to the animal and held her fingers in front of its nose. "It has to be a wolf. He's breathing. It's shallow. I'm going to feel for a heartbeat."

Trace winced before sticking her fingers through the blood matted fur on the animal's chest. "Barely there."

I brought the towel, got down on my knees next to him, and gently touched one of the only clean places, his ear. It was velvety soft, and the creature whimpered when I massaged it. I looked at Trace. "Aww. Poor thing. The ear is ice cold."

"Yeah, his whole body is," Trace affirmed. "We should at least wrap him up. He needs a soft place to rest until an expert can help."

I pulled out my cell and started a group text with David, Alder, and Micah:

> Hey, I haven't even had a chance to look for Will. There's an injured wolf (?) in the bottom of the damn pool! I mean, it's bad. He's barely alive. Must have escaped the zoo? What should we do?

As soon as the phone said Read, I received a barrage of replies from David:

WAIT.

DON'T CALL ANYONE.

CAN YOU GET HIM INSIDE?

"What the hell," I said out loud.

"What'd they say?"

"Oh my god. Is this some secret vampire shit? They want him inside." I sighed in exasperation.

Trace stood up. "Okay. I guess they know what they're talking about. Let me get a quilt or something we can drag him with. There's no way the two of us can pick him up. The thing is huge."

She brought one back as Marita walked up to the gate. "I brought you witches bells for the front door. What's with all the blood on the sidewalk out here?" She came inside and froze when she saw Trace's hands covered in red. "Are you two okay?"

I pointed to the pool. "Look. Do you know anything about wolves in New Orleans or maybe at the zoo?"

Her jaw dropped. "I...I might. Is it alive?"

"Yeah, but he's fading fast," Trace replied.

"David wants us to get it inside. I have no idea why we aren't calling animal control or someone," I said, frustration causing my voice to shake. My nerves were taking over and bewildered energy swirled within and all around me. I couldn't keep it from seeping through my skin. Trace put the quilt down beside the wolf and we struggled to slide him over. He yelped then whined when we pulled the sides up like a hammock. I stifled a scream at the horrid sound. I hated it when an animal was in pain.

"Wait. Where do we take him? David is in his house. Alder and Micah are over the shop in our place."

I quickly texted them again and they said to take the wolf to the shop. Trace and I pulled hard. Marita pushed the tail end. It took everything in us to drag him the short distance to the shop door. Who knew wolves were so heavy? I jumped when someone dressed in all black was suddenly behind Marita. All I could see were shining chocolate brown eyes. It was David, covered from head to toe. He moved past us, opened the door, and had the wolf inside with one easy swoop. The wolf cried out and I did too. I lost it. I was so tired from being up the entire night before, Will was still who knows where, and hearing this suffering soul was too much. I plopped down on the bottom step of the staircase with tears streaming down my face and watched David remove the black cloak and gloves. Then he began assessing the wolf. Was he some sort of veterinarian in the past, or what? He could have been many different things I wasn't aware of. Alder, Trace, and Marita stood by ready to help and Micah jogged downstairs and sat beside me with a secure arm around my shoulders. I began deep breathing and pushed the chaotic energy through the soles of my feet.

David raised one eyelid of the wolf then stuck an entire finger into the neck wound. He dug around and pulled out a large fang. "This is deep. Another wolf, maybe two attacked him." He soothed the poor animal. "I'm going to do everything I can to pull you through, mate." He petted the fur along his spine in smooth sweeps of his palm. "I'll need sutures and betadine if we can get it. Bandages too. Enough for a few days."

"I'm on it," Marita stated, then left.

My mind was running in circles. "Two wolves? Where are all of these wolves coming from? Is this a vampire thing? Can any of you explain? You all seem a little too calm."

"Willa," Micah scolded.

"What? This is crazy, right? And I should be looking for Will."

David whipped his head up frustrated and glared at me, sounding stern. "Look. Will might have shagged some lass and bunked down. Let me take care of the here and now, please."

His tone stung. Trace gave me somewhat of a smile. I ducked out from Micah's arm and went behind the bar to make coffee. It looked like we would be up for a good while longer. I watched David continue to pet and soothe the wolf.

Marita returned within the hour with everything he requested. I handed her a full mug of hot coffee. "Thank you for doing that," I sincerely told her. I was in no state to do anything. I felt helpless in the situation.

"Trace, can you assist me in cleaning and suturing the wounds? I'll need Alder and Micah to hold him down."

"Of course." Trace pulled on exam gloves and got to work.

"We will do this here, but he can't be thoroughly cleaned up until we know if he's going to survive. Alder, can someone from the clutch get antibiotics and pain medicine? At dusk, I'll take him to my place," David said.

"I'm sure we can."

I felt bad for being bitchy. "What can I do to prepare a spot for him to be comfortable over there?" I asked meekly.

"A sleeping bag would be ideal. Thank, you babe," David said in a much sweeter tone. He held my attention. "And I've not forgotten about Will. I promise."

"Okay," I mouthed.

I had fallen asleep on the sofa while they were working on the wolf. It took over two hours for every injury to be addressed. I woke up and Trace had gone back to her house to shower and rest with Harris. I yawned and stretched. Alder sat down and tucked me next to him.

"He won't leave the wolf's side," Alder said, referring to David. "Oh, and he wants you to know he heard from Will. He had an emergency. No further explanation, but I'm sure it must be important."

"Hmm, okay. He wouldn't just leave us like that."

"No, darling." Alder played with my hair. "You should go upstairs and sleep with Micah a little while longer."

I kissed his lips. "Alright, I'm easily persuaded."

I was still beat, and it would be a few more hours before sundown.

Eleven

DAVID

I spent time slowly combing dried blood from Will's fur. The thought that he may not make it cut me deeply, but that was the reality I faced. What if it came down to life or death? A glimmer in the back of my mind nagged that there could be one desperate option. The possibility was twisted. And would it even work? It had never been done before. *And* I had to tell Willa what was going on...eventually.

At dusk, Willa quietly came back into the café. She stood over my shoulder and ran her hands through my hair. I absorbed her soothing energy through my scalp. She pulled my head back and kissed me. I moaned. "God, I love you," my lips uttered against hers. Her tongue swiped across my bottom lip before her teeth gave it a tug.

"I love you, my wild one." Willa looked deep into my eyes. "David, I'm sorry I was...the way I was yesterday. I was shocked. Confused. But most of all...I felt helpless."

I shook my head. "No no, babe. No one expects you to know what to do all of the time. You are magical and strong and have become my light in this dark world, but you are also human. And you..." I wanted to touch her hair that had fallen onto my shoulder as she looked down at me, but my hands were still blood stained.

"You can cry, and you can scream. You can go fucking crazy on me, and I will always *always* stand by your side. I will hold your hand. I will wrap you up in love. I will pick you up and carry you if I must. I am yours, and you have three eternal immortal mates who will protect you at all costs."

Will snorted and licked his lips. Willa's eyes were compassionate. She reached down and rubbed his ear.

"I bet he's thirsty. Can we try giving him some water?"

I hopped up, but then raised my hands, realizing they were covered in dried blood.

"You go clean up, please. I'll sit with the wolf. Alder will be down in a minute. He can help me try to give him water." Willa looked stern. "I mean it. Go." She shoved me out the door.

WILLA

I threw a pillow from the sofa down beside the wolf. I didn't know how David had sat on the hard wood floor for so long. My knee was near the wolf's nose, and he sniffed it. Then panted a little. Alder and Micah trotted down the staircase.

"Good evening, darling. How's he fairing?" Alder asked.

"I don't know. I sent David to get a shower. I think the poor thing's thirsty. Can you please get me some water?"

Micah moved behind the bar in a flash.

"Hey, give me a paper towel too," I instructed.

I soaked the paper towel with water and squeezed a few drops onto the wolf's tongue. He grunted and took it eagerly. His eyelids lifted halfway, and he panted for more. I put my hand under his chin to guide his mouth to the bowl. I let him take half then laid his head back down. I watched his massive chest move up then back down with a big sigh. Alder sat down near the wolf's tail. I felt his eyes on me, and I looked at him.

"What are you thinking?"

His eyes went from me to the wolf. "I think you could help him more than you realize." Alder took my wrist and placed my hand flat on the wolf. His ribs were hard ridges under my fingers. "Send him some of your energy. Give him your healing magic."

Alder's hand was on top of mine, and he guided them across the wolf's fur together, avoiding the bandaged areas. There were so many.

"You have so much love inside you." Alder looked back at me. "He could use it right now."

I didn't think it was possible, but I cried again. This time, with a huge smile. I had a purpose in the chaos. I wiped the tears away with my clean hand then rubbed both thumbs over the wolf's eyebrows and down around his ears over and over several times. He groaned but sounded content. It felt good to him. It could only help. My hands glowed and I wrapped them the best I could around his huge paws. I sat there for a long time, until my posture slumped. Alder removed my hands and covered the wolf with a clean towel.

He pulled me to my feet, and I noticed my ass was numb. I wavered and he grabbed me around the waist. "You're drained. Micah's going to try his hand at shepard's pie."

My stomach rumbled at the thought. I had been in such a trance giving the wolf my energy that I hadn't noticed David, Harris, or Trace had all returned to the shop. Alder handed me over to Trace who led me to the sink to wash my hands, then to the sofa.

"Hey, Trace?"

"Yeah?"

"Will you make pancakes for dessert?"

She laughed. "Of course I will, bestie."

David came to me and pulled me onto his lap. He smelled like my bodywash when I nuzzled my nose under his chin, and he adjusted my position.

"Mmm, babe. Settle down," he laughed quietly. "We have to get you fed first."

Micah whistled out, signaling dinner was ready. It smelled amazing and I was starving. I moaned with the first bite then thought about Will. He would have eaten a whole pie by himself if he was here. Trace went to get seconds and stopped beside the wolf. His tail looked like it tried to wag a bit.

"Hey, I think he's hungry," Trace said.

The wolf panted again and grunted. Trace took the plate she just filled and sat beside him. David left the table to help. He gently lifted the wolf's head so he wouldn't choke. Trace used a spoon, and the wolf ate everything she offered. I brought more water, and he lapped it up. I rubbed his ear and Trace held his big paw, giving him more energy.

"I'm going to find a good healing spell for him," Trace stated. "He found us for a reason."

"Yeah, and maybe the vampires will tell us what they know soon," I whispered.

"They can hear you, ya know." She looked up and smiled at someone over my shoulder. I turned around and Micah winked.

David came over. "Thank you both for taking care of him and trusting me. There's no better place for him to be right now. I promise I won't keep you in the dark. After you offer him a spell, I will carry him over to my place."

DAVID

I laid Will down as gently as possible, but he whimpered in pain. Moving him wasn't ideal, but he couldn't remain at the cafe, and I wanted to keep my eye on him at all times. Thomas had dropped off the signed business plan along with the antibiotics and pain medicine I requested.

I patted Will's paw. "Rest, mate. I need you to get better. We all do. Everyone has taken a liking to you, you know. Well, maybe not Micah. I think he's a wee bit jealous." Will didn't move. I feared the worst, but I wouldn't let it show.

Willa came in and kissed my forehead then bent down and kissed Will's snout. "I hope the pain meds kick in quickly," she said. "Can I read this healing spell for him?"

"Please."

She held one huge paw in her hand.

Within my being, the wolf seeks relief
Body, mind, and spirit, find release
With gentle touch and soothing grace,
I heal the wounds, he finds his place

Energy flow, vibrant and strong,
Restoring health, where it went wrong
As I speak, so shall it be
A healed existence, I now decree

"Thank you, babe. Can you help me change the dressings? Just to hold him if it's too uncomfortable?"

"Of course." She smiled.

Willa didn't hesitate. She sat cross legged and cradled Will's head in her lap. He opened his eyes halfway and she rubbed his ears. She gasped a little every time I removed a bandage. It was bad. Every suture line was red, swollen and oozing. I used sterile water-soaked gauze to wipe away what I could, then we replaced the coverings.

Willa's hands shook a bit when she caressed Will's head. "I'm so sorry," she said to him. She looked at me. "I'm not sure he'll make it," she silently mouthed.

I pulled the sleeping bag over Will and zipped it up. "We will check on you in a bit. Sleep, mate."

I lifted Willa to her feet and took her to our bedroom. I heard her heart racing. She grabbed me around my waist, and I wrapped her up.

"It's too much. There's too much going on," she mumbled into my chest.

I lifted her chin. "Let it out. Let some of these emotions go. Don't keep the world on your shoulders."

Willa sighed. "I'm scared for the wolf. I'm excited about the shop. I feel bad that you are having to deal with all of this and I'm horny. And I feel bad for being horny with all of the other shit that's going on."

I couldn't help but laugh. I kissed her worried little face. I kissed her hard and her mouth desperately met my lips. I went feral when her tongue lustfully lapped at my descended fangs. We undressed each other and I threw her on the bed. I crawled on top, put my hand on her throat, and kissed her some more. She pulled my hips down and rocked hers up, grinding against my cock. It slid over her clit, and she moaned.

I kissed behind her ear and whispered. "We have to be quiet."

"Yes Sir," Willa giggled.

She had never called me Sir and it ignited something inside me. I bit her bottom lip. She gasped and ran her tongue over the taste of iron that now dripped down her neck. I read her mind, and she was okay with it, so I continued to satiate my craving. I started where the drip ended at her delicate collarbone. I licked slowly. Her skin vibrated, which excited me. Willa shivered as my tongue traveled up the blood trail to her bottom lip. I took it between my lips and sucked deeply. Willa rolled her pelvis under me, getting off on my cock against her clit. I abandoned the blood to feast on her breasts. Willa fisted her hand in my hair.

"Take more. Bite me, my wild one." She panted.

I happily obliged and my fangs sank into the soft side of her breast. Willa pulled my hips down as hard as she could and stifled a scream when she came.

"Fuck. Oh, David. Oh my god."

She held the back of my head as I continued to have my fill and rubbed my cock against her wet clit until cum spurted across her abdomen. I licked the wound and rolled off to lay next to her side as she played with my hair.

"I needed that."

"Mmm, me too babe."

Twelve

WILLA

Being with David definitely cleared the muddy energy. Although a lot of unknowns surrounded me, I felt lighter, and I knew I had many people by my side.

After a few hours of spooning and snoozing with him, I had to get up to relieve myself and needed a sip of water. I crept through the dark living room to the kitchen. I heard the wolf huff when I opened the refrigerator door. I took a swig of water and went to check on him.

I kneeled beside him and rubbed his ear like I had before. It was warm. Maybe too warm? I found his paw in the sleeping bag, and it burned. I was sure he had a fever. I rubbed my palm over his muzzle, and he opened his eyes. We stared at each other.

It felt familiar.

"Where did you come from?"

He tried to lick my nose and I laughed, but then he grunted and plopped his head back down. He needed something for the fever, I thought, but how the hell was I going to get a wolf to take Tylenol? I retrieved my industrial sized bottle, swiped my finger in some peanut butter and stuck two pills into the center of the blob. The wolf took it with no coercion and after cleaning my finger completely, he gave a light tug on the tip with his teeth. I couldn't believe I wasn't scared to have my hand in the mouth of a freaking wolf, but whatever secrets the vampires knew made me trust that he wouldn't hurt me.

"Hey, watch the teeth. You're a good boy, aren't you?" I sighed. "But you have to get better. And when you do, I guess we'll have a shop wolf instead of a shop cat. I mean, Trace and I have never been conventional witches, have we?"

"What are you two talking about," David asked as he propped against the door to his bedroom. He came and rubbed a hand down my hair. "I had to make sure you were okay and to check on him."

"I gave him Tylenol. I hope that's okay. He's burning up. It can't be a good sign."

David squatted beside us. "It's more than fine. I'm sure his temp is up from infection. The wounds don't look good, but I would rather him be hot than freezing cold. His body is fighting the infection and trying to heal. If he turns cold again...the body has given up and he won't last long."

I put my nose to the wolf's. "That's right. We want you a comfy cozy warm." I kissed his muzzle. "Go back to sleep, my good boy." Then I kissed David's cheek. "I need to wash the wolf slobber off my hand. You come back to bed soon."

"I'll be there in a minute, babe."

DAVID

Shit, the sun would be up within the hour, and I needed to rest, but Will's health was deteriorating. I hid my concern from Willa. I texted Alder and he and Micah were over in a flash. I put my finger to my pursed lips.

"Try to be quiet. Willa's still awake, and I don't want her out here."

Alder felt Will's hot paw. "What should we do? You know what would heal him."

I slowly nodded. "Yes, but you know if I give him my blood..."

"What?" Micah asked. "Surely he wouldn't change into a vampire shifter or something."

Alder laughed a little. "No, but a vampire has never given a shifter their blood. We don't know what could happen. With humans, the act solidifies the bond between mates. Or if a human is dying, it will heal them, but forces a mate-like connection. The human is attracted to the giver of the blood for the rest of their lives. The vampire would remain on their mind, even if they were separated by thousands of miles."

I sighed. "I don't want Will to die. I need him like I can't explain, but I don't want him to resent me for forcing a bond. Bonds are taken very seriously by shifters."

"Wait." Micah looked deep in thought. "What if he got out of control? What if he wanted more of your blood and attacked you or something? I might be way off, but—"

"No, you may be right." Alder rubbed his chin, thinking. "There's only one way to find out. If Will threatens you, he will be dealt with. It's up to you. It may be worth a try with him being so close to death. You can't wait until he dies. Then he really will be a vampire shifter something."

I put my hands on my hips. "Alright. Micah, make sure the windows are closed extra tight. Looks like I may be up all day again."

"You mean we." Alder placed a hand on my shoulder. "*We* are going to see this through."

I glanced at the bedroom door. "Oh, shit. What about Willa?"

We were silent, listening.

"Maybe she's asleep," Micah whispered.

"Okay, let's do this," I declared.

I placed Will's head in my lap while Alder and Micah watched. My fangs descended and I bit down on my wrist. Blood seeped out and I held it to his mouth. He lapped at the blood like water.

"I'm not sure how much to give him," I said. One drop may be just as effective as a mouth full. I didn't know. I had never given anyone my blood.

"What the fuck are you doing?" Willa exclaimed.

Her face twisted and I jerked my wrist to my chest to hide the bite. "Willa, it's okay."

Alder was next to her in a flash and held her arm. "David's helping him. The wolf wouldn't survive."

She pulled back with wide eyes. "So? It's a *wolf*! What is so damn important about this wild animal? Is this like a familiar thing? I want to know-I deserve to know why the wolf is drinking your blood, David."

I pulled the sleeping bag over Will's back and tried to think of what to say.

She turned to Micah. "Do you know what's going on?"

"Yuh, yes," he stuttered.

Alder spoke up. "It will heal the wolf. He was in too much pain and antibiotics take too long. He was not going to make it through the day."

I went to Willa. "Do you trust me?"

She nodded silently.

I searched her eyes. "Trust me."

She looked at each of us and relaxed her shoulders. "Ugh! All of you! It should be against vampire law to make a human so horny at a time like this!"

"Damn, Willa." Micah laughed and put his hand on the back of her neck. She riled him up.

"Well, it's true. It's hard for me to be in the same room with all of you at the same time."

Alder kissed Willa's lips softly. "Why don't you and Micah go have it out then and get some sleep after?"

Micah swiftly picked her up off of her feet and she squealed. "You don't have to tell me twice." He smiled wickedly as he turned and carried her to the bedroom. She made no protest and was already kissing him before he closed the door.

Alder and I turned our attention to Will. He panted and I gave him water. I took the cover off and his tail lifted up and flopped back down with hard thumps a few times. Signs of life. I leaned down and put my forehead to his velvety one.

"Don't be mad at me when you pull through this. And...please don't eat me."

Alder patted my back. "You have back up if he bloody tries."

"Have you ever given your blood to a human to heal them? One this close to death?" I asked Alder.

71

"I have. I had a relationship with a man for a decade in the 1920's. A now long forgotten epidemic infected over one million people throughout the world and killed about half of that number. They called it the sleeping sickness. It attacked the brain. One day he was perfectly healthy, the next he lay motionless in the bed unable to speak. I loved him. I gave him my blood."

"It took three days for him to rouse, but he would only look at me blankly. The worst part was...I could still read his mind and his thoughts had no good in them. He was very aware of what was going on. I kept on loving him and took care of him, bathed him and changed his soiled linens. He kept asking me telepathically to hire a caretaker, to leave him. I refused. When he didn't improve after a month, he began begging me to kill him. Over and over he chanted and pleaded in my head. It was tortuous to my soul. I knew he wasn't my fated mate, but he was the only human I had loved since my wife who died in London from the Black Death in the time before I was a vampire. It wasn't easy knowing Willa would eventually be my forever mate and waiting so long for her. Vampires have many loves and losing them never gets any easier. When Willa is turned, I will finally feel complete."

I felt for Alder. I hadn't lost any loves until now. I guess I did love Will. If he died, a part of me would die. I loved Willa too. Life was getting very interesting.

"So, it could take a while for him to have the strength to shift," I mused. "I hope it works. God, I hope it works."

"We should probably drink some Vena since we aren't getting any rest today," Alder said.

We sat on the sofa and talked until dark. Alder told me about the first time he met Willa and Micah. Speaking of Micah, he sauntered out of the bedroom in his boxer briefs and made a bee line for the fridge. He downed a glass of Vena and raised the empty glass to us. "I didn't drink from Willa. Figured she was too tired for that. Well, she's definitely too tired after ravaging my body the way she did."

"Pshh," Alder scoffed. "That magical human is a lot more powerful than any of us can imagine. My beautiful mate. *Our* beautiful mate. You two better thank the universe you have her, or that she'll have you."

"Every damn day," Micah added. He plopped down, squeezing between us on the sofa. We only laughed at him. Micah knew how to make any situation lighter. He turned to me. "So, when's the next fashion show? I'm a model, you know."

I smiled. "Yes, you've mentioned it. You're gorgeous. I'd be chuffed to have you on my catwalk."

"Eeny, meeny, miny, moe," Willa joked, tapping each of us on the back of our heads. She touched mine last and I grabbed her wrist. She gasped in surprise as I pulled her down across our laps.

I growled. "If us vampires weren't so spent, and there wasn't a wolf watching..."

"Mmm," she hummed and snuggled into us. "Is the blood working?"

Alder rubbed her pretty feet. "In time."

Wait. I sniffed the air. Alder read my mind and he stood up and walked to the front door, making sure it was locked. I jumped up and Willa stayed in Micah's lap.

"You catch that scent too?" I asked Alder.

"Yes," he grumbled. A fierce light flashed in his eyes. "Let's go before they're on the move and get away."

Micah practically dumped Willa onto the floor. "I'm coming too."

"No, stay here," Alder ordered.

"No way. You think there are two of them, right? The more of us the better."

Alder hesitated. "Fuck. Alright. I'll get Harris too." He looked at a frightened Willa. "Trace can come sit with you and Wi...the wolf."

Willa huffed. "Okay, maybe one day you'll tell me what's going on." Then she softened. "Be careful."

She got three big hugs before we left.

Thirteen

WILLA

I double checked that I had locked the door after Trace entered. She held up two big travel mugs.

"Hot cocoa from scratch." Trace smiled.

"Oh my god, thank you. Let's sit and sip. So, did you hear? David gave the wolf his blood," I asked.

"Yeah. I tried to get the truth out of Harris, but he won't tell me why the wolf is so important."

We both looked over at the big lump under the sleeping bag. There was movement, almost like a shivering. Trace and I screamed when we saw the hand of a man reach over the top edge and pull it tighter up over itself.

"Oh shit," Trace whispered, and we jumped up and backed against the opposite wall near the bedroom door. The wolf or man was too close to the front door. We would have to run into the bedroom if need be.

I panted, freaking out. "Trace...I think we may find out what's so fucking important about the wolf. Go look."

Her wild-eyed face whipped to mine. "You go look! He's your vampire's...thing."

My chest heaved and my heart knocked against my ribcage as I tiptoed toward where he lay. The floorboards creaked and I froze when a low growl rumbled from his chest. I felt it through the bottom of my feet. I looked at Trace in anticipation. The swish of the sleeping bag being thrown off had me turning on my heels to face what I feared. Within seconds a naked man covered in bandages and dried blood crouched, ready to pounce. I recognized his eyes. Trace ran to my side. I held her hand and squeezed it. "Wait. It's Will."

He looked startled and confused. His eyes stayed on me. He growled again. I didn't like it. If he lashed out, we were no match for his strength. Oh shit, I thought. Especially with vampire blood.

I moved the energy swirling inside my core to my hands. They glowed and his face changed from feral to interest. I took a step closer, and he lunged at me. Trace screamed again and flattened herself back against the wall. I jumped toward the front door, but he was faster and put himself in front of it so quickly, his body stopped me like a brick wall. It hurt like one too. His hands grabbed my arms and held me against his chest. Will still panted excitedly. He leaned in and sniffed my hair. Then his nose skimmed down my jawline to my neck. I prayed he wouldn't bite down and tear out my jugular. I felt an exhale of warm breath.

"Oh, Willa."

His hands released my arms and wrapped around me so tight, and he cried, pulling us both down to the floor. I held on and cradled him close with his head tucked under my chin. "It's okay. It's going to be okay," I soothed.

Will sat back, looked down, and covered himself. "Fuck. I'm sorry. Did I scare you? I didn't mean to scare you." He glanced over his own body. "I'm okay."

"Yes. Yes, you are. And you need a shower and something to eat," I told him.

He smiled meekly. "Yeah, I do."

"I'll cook something up," Trace declared.

I pushed Will to his bedroom and noticed a wolf head tattoo on his shoulder. "You okay to clean yourself up?"

"Maybe." He smiled wickedly.

"You'll be alright. Go. I'm texting David."

DAVID

Harris held Levi face down with his blood covered boot planted on the middle of his back. Rafe's blood. Levi pleaded and begged for us to spare his life after he witnessed the slaughter of Rafe. The two hadn't been hard to find. The wounds from the fight with Will reeked of weeping puss. Both were weak and we caught them by surprise. They had broken into an empty house for sale two doors down from our place to sleep for the night. Alder dealt a harsh punishment. I witnessed a side to him I never knew existed and I think Micah was taken aback by how tortuous Alder had been with Rafe. He used his fingers to rip the previous wounds open further and blood poured from every gash. Alder shoved a filthy bandage down Rafe's throat so he couldn't scream out when he took his dagger to Rafe's tattoo. Every shifter had one. I had seen Will's. He wore it with pride. A black wolf head on back of his right shoulder. Rafe growled and choked when Alder sliced into his skin with the tip of the dagger, pushing in and going deeper than needed for the task and as slow as possible for maximum effect. Levi whimpered while he watched, and Micah told him to shut up. I stepped back a bit, so the growing pool of blood didn't get on my shoes. Knowing the fucker who almost killed Will suffered and died pitifully and in agony, strangling and suffocating on his own putrid puss, gave me a hard on. It was fucking twisted. Alder smirked and held up the chunk of flesh dripping with blood and fatty adipose to show Levi.

"I think I'll let Will take yours if he even wants to bother with it," he said maliciously.

Alder wiped his hands the best he could on his black jeans and pulled out his cell. The Hunt clutch would clean up the mess and take Levi to a discreet holding place to be dealt with later. We needed to get back to the house.

The four of us stopped on the front porch to remove our boots. Will had heard our arrival and made it out before anyone else. He burst through the door looking perfectly healed and full of life and he tackled me. I could hardly believe it. My blood worked. Fast. We hugged each other hard, and the others went inside. I pulled back to see his face. He smiled and blushed. "Hey, boss."

"You're okay."

"I'm okay," he said. "Thank you for saving me. I know what you did. And the unknowns of it all."

Will's eyes flashed from brown to gold and something within me changed. He looked different. Like I could stare at him forever. He smelled different. Sweeter. I wanted to be near him.

"It's your blood," he said quietly. "I..."

"We'll figure it out, mate," I assured him. "Is Willa okay?"

"Of course. I could never hurt her. I scared the shit out of her and Trace though. At first. I was confused. We all were." He looked down at his feet. "Is Levi..."

"Rafe is dead. Levi is in holding."

Will's head snapped up. "So, you didn't kill him?" He looked surprised.

"That's your call, mate. I'll execute him if that's what you feel he deserves. You wouldn't have to do it."

"Oh, he fucking deserves it. But I think an extended vacation at Castle Blair for a few months would be fitting."

"Do you wish to see him first?"

"I don't know if I ever want to see him again. Fuck him." The dark mood passed over Will's face. "Let's go in. I'm sure Willa's waiting for you."

Willa held onto Micah since Alder was still covered in blood. Alder and Harris were trying to explain to Willa and Trace what happened. Willa reached for me, and I took her hand.

"We don't have a protection agreement here in New Orleans, but the clutch has never ruled it out," Alder said. "I'm not aware of a shifter community here, but Will may be able to shed more light on that."

Will paced the floor. He was beautiful and his stride reminded me of a wolf surveying his pack.

"There aren't many of us in London because wolves aren't native there. I'm David's protector, so that's where I am. I go where he goes. Communities are not surprisingly called packs. Members who don't have protection agreements live where real wolves are safest. Mountains or thick forests on the outskirts of cities and urban neighborhoods. It isn't hard integrating with humans when you can control the shifting."

"Well, you're very good at keeping your secrets," Trace said. "I'm surprised the covens don't know about this. And please know, I promise to keep your secrets safe."

"Oh, some witches know," Will replied. "I think it depends on where we live. If a pack member gets injured and can't change back to human, we often seek out witches for help. We can't show up at the emergency room or a veterinarian, for that matter. Even if we are injured in human form, we often still go to witches. If a lab draws blood, they see a difference and all kinds of questions are raised."

Will went to Willa and gently touched her cheek. "I'm sorry I've brought all of this into your life. I put you in danger and I hated that you didn't know the whole truth. David didn't know how to tell you."

"It's not your fault," I stated. "I take the blame alone. You... you almost died." I fought back tears. "But if we hadn't been here with Willa and Trace, and all of you..." I let go of Willa's hand and took both of Will's. "If Rafe and Levi had attacked you in London, you may not have survived, and I needed the help of Alder and Harris and Micah. I will be forever grateful to the Hunt clutch."

Will softened and looked at Willa again. "I felt you. The energy you and Trace gave me kept me from tumbling over the edge and into darkness." He turned to me. "Thank you for your blood, boss."

"Speaking of blood," Alder's voice boomed. "I'm still covered in it. I know it's hours before the sun comes up, but we have all been running on adrenaline. Let's clean up and turn in. Willa and Trace have deliveries tomorrow night for the shop."

He kissed Willa's cheek and Micah hugged her. "Sleep well," Micah said and kissed her forehead.

Fourteen

WILLA

David got in the shower, and I fell onto his bed. My mind stayed on Will who was alone in his room. I wanted to hold him and just be with him to offer comfort but had no idea what David would say. I tossed and turned. I huffed and puffed and finally threw off the comforter.

I went to Will's door and barely knocked. I had decided that if he didn't hear it, he was asleep, and I would let it go. His voice came through the door, straight into my chest. My body vibrated.

"Willa," he grumbled hoarsely.

I slowly opened the door and peeked in. Will sat on the edge of his bed in green plaid pajama pants and no shirt with his elbows on his knees and his head in his hands. He raised up and his darkened brown eyes glinted gold for a second. I didn't speak. I went to him and held his head on my tummy. He wrapped his arms around my waist, and I massaged energy through my hands into his scalp. He sighed.

"Come with me," I instructed and led him to David's room. He laid down on my side and I got in the middle and spooned him. He needed it and I hoped David would understand.

Within a couple of minutes, Will went to sleep. David walked out of the bathroom naked and froze when he saw Will. I leaned up on my elbow and put my finger to my lips. "He's out," I whispered. "Please don't be mad. I'll wake him and send him back to his room if you want."

David put on boxer briefs and curled up behind my back. His arm snaked around me, and he put his nose to my ear. "Thank you for taking care of him." David's lips moved against my neck. "Even when you thought he was an escaped zoo animal, you let him in." David kissed my shoulder.

"Well, next time, let me in on the secret a little sooner." I got serious. "I trust you, David." I laced my fingers with his and pulled him closer. "My wild one."

I blinked a few times and remembered I had gone to bed with both David and Will when my vision acclimated to the dark and I saw Will's peaceful face and pretty brown curls that fell over his brow. I smoothed them over and he smiled but kept his eyes closed.

"I'm not ready to get up," he mumbled.

I kissed his nose. "Don't. The sun will still be up for about a half hour. Stay with David."

I scooted out from between them and left them quiet and still. I freshened up, dressed in comfy sweats, and went over to the shop.

I enjoyed a cup of coffee alone. I couldn't wait to try our After Dark brand. Thomas would be by in a few hours with samples, and pub tables and chairs were to be delivered as well. When the sun fell behind the skyline, I opened the shutters and looked out at the street. A whoosh of air flew up behind me and Alder wrapped his arms around my waist. His nose sniffed my braid.

"Good evening, darling."

I turned to taste his lips. He was my destiny, my security, my home. Our tongues caressed and played, and I moaned into his mouth when I felt fangs. I pulled him away from the window so we wouldn't be on display. Alder backed me up against the door, leaned on the solid wood, and licked up the side of my neck so slowly, I almost came. The top three buttons of Alder's dress shirt were undone, and his sleeves were rolled up, showing off his forearms. Fuck me. I needed a new thong that wasn't wet.

"You're panting. Mmm. I like that. Be a good girl and give me a taste. Will you let me drink? Will you quench my thirst?"

He knew I was very willing, and I would never deny him. I pressed my thighs together, trying to control myself. Alder held my jaw in his firm grasp and turned my chin to one side. I closed my eyes, anticipating his next move. He put his lips to my ear and drew out the word he said slowly and sensually.

"Mine."

My knees went weak, and he held me up with a strong arm while fangs sank in. No one compared to him. Yes, I had other mates who I couldn't imagine living without, and it seemed the number was growing, but Alder was the center of my universe and that would never change.

He had his fill and licked the wound. I held him in place. I wanted to stay close. He nuzzled into me again.

"Don't ever forget."

"Forget what," I asked.

"That you're mine," Alder growled through gritted teeth.

"Hey, you two," Micah gleefully said as he trotted down the steps.

Alder straightened up and turned, but I took a hold of his wrist, and he looked back.

"Forever."

DAVID

Will grumbled and stretched his long legs but didn't open his eyes. I lay on my stomach, watching him. He was two inches taller than me and had more bulk. So strong. A perfect protector. When his feet touched mine, his eyes opened, and a hint of a smile touched his lips.

"Hi, boss."

"How'd you sleep? Feel rested?"

"Yes, thanks to you and Willa. I hope you don't mind. She practically forced me into your bed," he joked.

I laughed. "Ah, well, she couldn't leave you in there alone after everything that happened." I got up and slid on my trousers. "And you won't be in our bed every night," I added.

Will nodded. "Noted."

He got up and helped me make the bed, then went to get dressed.

"I'll see you at the shop, boss," he said when I left.

Vampires who I assumed were members of the Hunt clutch unloaded chairs from a box truck parked at the front door of the shop, so I went through the courtyard to see if I could help. Each one tipped their heads down and called me sir. It was easy to forget who I was here in the States. I held my head a little higher. I was the primus of London and should project that image.

Thomas jumped down from the back of the truck. He had been directing the operation.

"Good evening, Mr. Kingswood. Such an honor to see you again." He bowed to me.

I touched his elbow and straightened him up.

"Thomas, there's no need for such formality. I feel like we are all just a big family, truthfully. I want to help. What can I do?"

"Oh, nonsense, sir. You just go in and…"

I smiled, walked past him, and leapt up into the trailer to grab a pub table, easily lifting it, and carried it inside. I winked at Willa as I set the table down inside and continued to help until we emptied the truck.

A representative from a restaurant supply company instructed Willa, Trace, Micah, and a few other vampires who had expressed an interest in working at the café how to use the commercial machine. Alder handed me and Thomas glasses of Vena and we watched. Will ordered Chinese for the humans and himself. Of course Alder spared no expense and purchased a high-end Enigma system along with a Nitro and cold brew dispenser. He said the Bloody Good blend needed special filtration. There was a lot more to owning a coffee shop than I had pictured.

We waited for Trace and Willa to place the tables and chairs exactly where they wanted. A van delivered cases of coffee and we all fussed over the packaging.

Willa lifted the first whole bean coffee bag from the box and kissed it. She passed it around. It was a matte black flat-bottom bag. The logo, in neon pink, said *After Dark* with a tarot card graphic. The Bloody Good blend had to be freeze-dried instant because of the infused blood. The logo was in red with a realistic bat graphic on the same matte black bag.

"Perfect," Alder commented.

"Yes! So perfect," Trace squealed. "Marketing is *so* important, and these couldn't have turned out better. The store front signage and menu board should arrive this week."

"It's getting real," Willa mused while she looked around the place.

Alder stood behind her and massaged her shoulders. "Brilliant."

Fifteen

WILLA

After we situated the café and ate take out, our vampire helpers from the clutch left with Thomas. David and Alder sat side by side at the piano and played lively music. Harris and Trace laughed as they twirled around the floor.

Will answered a knock at the door and it was Marita.

"It's midnight. Are you keeping vampire hours now?" I teased.

"Midnight shmidnight. I'm a night owl. I heard the music on my way home, and I wanted to bring you a little something for the counter of the café."

Will smelled the purple flowers and green leaves.

"Violets and clover," he said.

Marita looked surprised. "Very good. Violets will boost positive spiritual energy and clover promotes luck, wealth, and success."

I took them. "Teach me, Marita. I really should learn more about magical herbs. I'm not a very good witch."

"You're a fine witch, but I would love to teach you everything I know."

Will turned to Marita and held out a hand. "Would the witch fancy a dance with the wolf?"

"Okay," she answered hesitantly, and they glided over to Harris and Trace.

Marita laughed and gave into the whimsy of it all. I felt happiness welling up within me. Not that I wasn't happy before, but it was met with the sense of accomplishment and pride in the café and togetherness of everyone that I loved. There were still a lot of unknowns, but in this moment, we were safe.

I stuck my nose to the violets and Will returned to me after the dance.

"They smell good, don't they," he said. He placed his hand on mine that was flat on the counter and rubbed his thumb across my knuckles. I turned it over and laced our fingers together.

"Am I out of place?" he genuinely asked.

I glanced at Micah leaning against the piano. I felt his attention trained on us. Micah looked away quickly. I could tell he was jealous. I looked back at Will and spoke quietly.

"There's no way around this. I know we've bonded. And believe me when I say, I'm not upset about it now. I don't feel stuck in a situation I don't want to be in. Alder and David know it can't be ignored, but Micah...he's going to have a hard time with it. You and I have to take it slow. I'll never hurt him in any way."

"I would never want you to. This isn't easy for me either. In my mind, I always thought I would bond with another shifter; have one mate, but you live in a world I've never imagined. I'm not complaining. I just feel like I'm stepping on a lot of toes. Vampire toes, to be exact. And my boss' mate? It's barmy, innit?"

I laughed. "If that means crazy, yes, yes, it is."

Will let go of my hand. "You should go talk to him."

I kissed Will's cheek and looked at Micah when I walked by, signaling him to follow me upstairs to his and Alder's apartment. He was behind me in a flash with his hand on the small of my back.

Alder decorated the unit with the furniture from his previous home. I made Micah sit on the crimson velvet sofa. The same one where he, Alder, and I had discussed our arrangement at the beginning of all of this. Where Alder kissed him the first time. I would never forget that.

"That was a great night," he said, reading my thoughts. "I miss it. The three of us."

I snuggled up as close as I could beside him. "And being human?"

He held me tight with his chin on the top of my head.

"No. I wouldn't be here if I was a human. Wesley would have killed me easily. Cateline too."

"But if I hadn't brought you into all of this..."

"Willa. Stop. Don't even go there. I wouldn't change anything, but—"

"Anything but Will," I said.

Micah sighed and I put my hand over his heart. The slow steady beat calmed me, and I sent loving energy to him. "What about David?"

"David fits. He makes sense and I'm pretty fond of him myself now, but the wolf..."

I drummed my fingertips on his chest. "Yes, the wolf."

Micah pressed his lips to my head. "I'm extremely jealous."

I leaned back to look at him, my beautiful blond immortal Adonis. "You don't hide it well. Don't get me wrong, it's flattering." I climbed onto Micah's lap. "Will doesn't want to cause turmoil or an upheaval of our lives. He's confused too and he knows you're not happy about it."

Micah set his mouth into a line. "Good."

I scoffed. "Micah!"

He grabbed my chin. "No one's ever taking you away from me. I swear, Willa. I feel very territorial, and I won't hide it."

I kissed his mouth hard. Kiss after kiss after kiss. I leaned back when he moaned. "Don't hide it. You wanting me makes me all hot and bothered and, fuck, let's go."

He laughed. "Go? Where?"

"Throw me on the bed. Let's. Go."

My body was under Micah, pressed into the mattress in two seconds.

WILL

Marita was a delight. We sat at the café counter, and she told me all about how everything went down with Cateline and Leona. They had all been through so much and kept coming out stronger on the other side. I admired them.

"Willa and Trace are special. You can easily see why everyone is drawn to them. I'm honored to be considered a friend and spiritual counselor," she said wistfully.

"Yeah, I find myself unexpectedly involved. I think you may understand where I'm coming from?"

She smiled. "I do. Don't lose heart. It may take some time, but things will always work out."

I leaned nearer. "I'll try to have patience."

David joined us, sliding onto the stool next to Marita. She practically swooned over him, but I had gotten used to everyone being taken with the famous model.

"Mr. Kingswood. It's great to see you again. Don't you love what the girls have done with the place? It's going to be so popular."

"Please, call me David." He smiled. "And, yes, what better city to have a vampire coffee shop and tarot parlor? I was never going to convince Alder to open a sex club."

"He tried many times." I winked at Marita.

"Speaking of," David said, retrieving his cell from his pocket. "I should give Ian a ring to check on Lust and tell him Castle Blair will have a new tenant for a few months." He patted my shoulder and went out on the café porch.

My eyes followed Willa as she walked down the staircase with Micah close behind. He shot a cocky grin my way and they came to join us. I knew they had sex. I smelled it on them and wished it'd been me with her. One day, I told myself. I was so glad the vampires couldn't read my mind.

David returned and Alder poured more Vena for the vampires. Alder held up his glass.

"It's a great night to celebrate. Will was not lost. After Dark is coming together and everyone I love is here."

"Here, here," Harris cheered before taking a long swig. Willa and Trace clinked wine glasses together.

"All is well in London?" I asked David.

"Oh, yes, but I know we have to go back next week, and I don't want to think about leaving Willa. I miss the club and the clutch, but..."

"I know what you mean," I said. "And my drama took center stage. I'm sorry about that, boss."

"Hey, we made it through, mate and we'll figure out the future. I've decided not to stress over it. I think I like this thing between us. I'm not sure what to do with it yet, but I fancy it."

David was beautiful and our mutual attraction grew by the second.

Willa appeared between us. "I wanted to thank you both."

"For what," I asked.

"For going with the flow. You never know what to expect when I'm around. I'm talking about the bonding shit."

"You've had, let me guess...three drinks, haven't you," David stated more than asked.

Willa giggled. "Hmm, maybe." She propped an arm on each of our shoulders. Her eyes went back and forth between us. "You bonded with me. You gave him your blood and now he's bonded with you. It's all a little fucked up, isn't it?" Willa got distracted from her ramblings and picked up David's half full glass of Vena. "What if I drank this?"

It almost made it to her lips before he grabbed it.

"Willa, stop. It wouldn't do anything to you. It would probably just taste like shit."

She pouted. Drunk Willa was a handful. She looked at Alder. "When are you going to turn me?"

His face showed annoyance. "Not now, and certainly not when you're drunk," he scolded.

Willa huffed, then took a bow. "Well, now you all know I'm not perfect. Sometimes I'm a mess," she slurred before heading outside to the courtyard. David held up a finger to everyone and followed her. "I've got this."

Sixteen

WILLA

I stumbled out of the door and into the dark early morning hours. David's fingers dug into my waist as he steadied me.

"Where are you off to?"

"Your place," I answered like he should know the answer. "Are you angry with me too?"

"Who's angry with you?"

"Alder gets pissed at me when I drink too much, which I totally get, and Micah's jealous of Will who is probably upset he didn't bond with another shifter. And you. This was supposed to be a vacation with loads of fucking."

He stopped and spun me around, looking down at my face. "That's not what I came for." His grip now tight on my wrist. "Okay, not *all* I came for. Willa, you're like a whirlwind. You rush in and fill every space around me. You refresh my spirit and calm me. You bring the air into my lungs and make me feel so alive. You lift me up and carry me. Make no mistake, where the wind blows, I follow."

I stood straighter. David's words sobered me up. I pulled his mouth down to meet mine and he hugged me close, breathing me in.

His mischievous eyes twinkled like stars when he looked at me.

"I want to take you back to the hotel tomorrow night for some alone time without Will being in the next room."

He swept me off my feet and carried me inside. "Today, we rest."

David deserved more of me. London called to him, and he would have to leave soon. I had to make our time alone all about him.

When we stepped into the hotel elevator, I stood across from him, not letting him touch me. Not yet. He licked his lips with fire in his eyes, surveying the way the shiny red satin caressed my curves.

"You're driving me mad," he grumbled.

David's gaze followed my every move when we entered the suite. I flipped on a couple of lamps and told him to stand at the foot of the king-sized bed. He adjusted his cock, and I asserted my dominance over him by batting his hand down to his side.

"Did I tell you to touch yourself?"

"No," he answered quietly. He lifted his chin and looked down at me through squinted eyes. His brow furrowed and he fisted his hands.

I slid my hands under his black tee, helping it over his head. David threw it on the floor. He gasped when I unbuckled the belt and let it slide around his waist painfully slow. His chest moved up and down with excited breaths and I instructed him to get naked. I pushed him onto the edge of the bed and pointed out the full-length mirror on the wall across from where he sat.

I stepped between his knees, facing the mirror, and slid out of my dress and lacey lingerie. My eyes watched David's eyes in the mirror's reflection, and I put my hair in a long ponytail before I turned around to face him. He looked up at me with so much desire. I leaned over his shoulder to get a bed pillow and felt his nose skim the sensitive skin over my ribs as he took in my scent. It lit my fire.

The pillow landed on the floor with a thud, and I went down on my knees between his legs. David's fangs were on display, and I loved turning him on in ways he never expected. My hands moved up his thighs and he moaned. His cock throbbed when I wrapped my hand around it and his body strained at the touch of my tongue over the tip. I pulled back and directed one of his hands to cup my breast.

David squeezed it and hissed, "Willa."

I moved his hand to my hair. He grasped my ponytail and gave it a tug. I returned my eager mouth to his cock and sucked until my jaws hurt. David was so close to the edge, so I stopped. He panted and tried to move my mouth back down. Not yet.

"Let go," I said firmly.

"Babe," he pleaded but let go of my hair.

I stood, pushed David down on the mattress, and straddled his hips. He lifted his pelvis up against my clit and I couldn't help but whimper, grinding into it. I put his hands on my hips, and he guided my body along perfectly with each move he made until I stopped him again before I went over the edge.

David growled, "Babe, let me."

I hushed him with my mouth and let my tongue feel his fangs. I wanted them. I wanted David to bite me and drink me while he took what was his. I was all his in that moment.

I looked at his perfect face. "My wild one." My fingers traced his lips. "I love you, David."

He sat up, holding me so tight around my waist while he kissed me. Then he flipped me down on the bed and was inside me so fast. He looked into my eyes, but steadily thrusted in and out as pleasure built.

"Can I taste you, Willa, please?"

He already knew my answer. His lips dipped down to my neck and fangs sank into flesh.

DAVID

I treasured resting with Willa until sunset. Her hands never left me as an Uber drove us back to Esplanade. I absorbed the energy her palms emitted every place she touched. She kissed me over and over and I held her close a few more moments before getting out.

"I hope you loved it," she said between kisses.

"Of course I did. You were bloody brilliant."

We walked hand in hand into the café and noticed Will sitting in the tarot parlor with Trace. A beaded curtain the colors of purple, green, and gold provided the only barrier in the wide doorway. She flipped over a few cards in front of him on the table. He sensed us and looked over. I nodded and Willa and I joined the others at the café counter. We didn't want to pry. Readings were very personal.

Willa hugged Micah then kissed Alder's cheek.

"I'll be at a clutch meeting for a bit tonight. Nothing pressing. It's just been a while," Alder stated. "Don't let her drink too much," he told Micah before he walked out the door.

Willa's mouth gaped open for a second then closed. Her good mood dipped, and I could see hurt on her face. She huffed, "I'm going to your place, David. Alone. I need to decompress."

I took her hand, but it slid out of my grasp as she gave me a weak smile and left.

I got three glasses out and poured Vena. "Can we talk?" I asked Harris and Micah. "What was all that about? Drinking hasn't been a big problem with Willa as far as I'm aware. Alder might need to be easier on her."

"Alder's nervous. He may not let it show, but I can tell every time Willa mentions being turned, he gets moody," Harris said.

Micah agreed. "I know he made her mad last night and apparently just now, but we talked about why after you two went to the hotel."

"Okay, enlighten me."

"The only two things that I have ever seen Alder get snappy about are threats to someone he loves and fear. I think he's afraid of her magic if it is amplified as a vampire."

"It makes sense and I totally get it," Harris said.

"Well, yes, you would understand." I nodded. "What does Trace think? Does she talk about being a vampire?"

Harris smiled. "A lot. She thinks she's ready. I can't fucking wait, but I want her to be a hundred percent sure."

Will held the bead curtain to the side for Trace and they joined us.

"Where's Willa? You two have fun last night?" Will asked.

The image in the mirror of Willa on her knees flashed through my mind. "It was...fantastic, mate. She's over at our place."

"Is she okay?" Trace asked. "Alder's tone was a bit harsh with her last night. I was surprised."

No one else answered so I did. "I think so." Trace looked concerned. "She will be," I added.

Harris kissed her cheek. "I'll talk to my brother when he returns. I know he would never intentionally hurt her."

"Never," Micah stated. "Willa is his everything."

Will bit his lip nervously before speaking up.

"I want you to know, I don't wish to change what you all have. Coming here has been eye opening. Hell, meeting Willa the first time in London blew my mind. Things have only escalated, as we all know."

He paused when Alder walked in the front door of the cafe. "Go ahead. I need to hear this too."

"Same," Willa said from where she leaned against the back door.

Will began to pace, then stopped and sighed before continuing. "I had never bonded with another shifter...or human." He looked at Willa. "Or vampire before coming here." He looked at me. "I genuinely thought if I didn't start a life with a shifter, I would be alone and live as David's protector. That's all the universe had to offer me." His gaze landed on Willa again. "But I was brought to my knees in that moment when we arrived in front of your old place. Even in front of David. Time stood still and the world faded away except for you. I thought about running. Running from what I thought was impossible and what I thought could never be. Running because you weren't mine. The night Rafe and Levi attacked me, I was going to stay away unless David needed me. I think. I was going to at least try to stay away, but then I brought all of my problems right back here to all of you, because I had nowhere else to go."

Will looked so vulnerable and humble and I wanted to comfort him. "Will, I brought you here for fucks sake. None of this is your fault. I told you that. I won't let you take the fall for any of it. You have never been an outsider. Not to me."

"Not to me either," Willa said quietly.

Trace spoke up. "The reading I did for Will confirmed the events that have already been set into motion. For you both," she said to Willa and me.

"How do you know it was meant to reflect us both?" Willa asked.

"I drew twice, first setting my intention on you. The second reading set on David. The same three cards were pulled in the exact same order. Can I share, Will?"

Will nodded.

"The Lovers and Two of Cups mean passionate soulmate love, real and on a karmic level which would represent the shifter bond. Then the Empress. The bond is selective and elevated. You know, the magnetic pull for one another. There's no reason to seek out relationships because fate decides. It was a powerful reading and when the second mirrored the first, I got goosebumps."

Alder walked straight to Willa and held her against himself. "I'm so sorry for the way I behaved. I was unkind and severe. Please, forgive me, my darling."

She looked up at him. "I'm yours, Alder."

He kissed the tip of her nose and turned to Will. "I would be lying if I said I comprehended what kind of bond a shifter has with, well anyone, but I do understand that each person who comes into our lives is meant to. I admit that I am afraid of what kind of power Willa will have as a vampire, but maybe it's going to take all of us to rein it in." He laughed but got serious in his next breath. "I think I just need everyone to know that we all have a place, but no one will ever take my place."

Alder had staked his claim, and I didn't blame him. I knew my place and was content to be there.

"And we are thankful the universe allows us to share a little part of your world. It's going to be fucking hard to go back to London in a couple of days," I said with a sigh.

Willa looked at me and Will. "You're a bigger part than you think. I'm not sure where it comes from, but I have a lot of love to give."

Seventeen

WILLA

Before I got the words out of my mouth, Micah was out the front café door in a flash. I ran onto the porch, but he was gone. Alder was by my side in an instant.

"He needs to think. Blow off steam. Micah will be back."

I sat on the top step. "I know. He promised he would never leave me. Or you, you know."

Alder ran a hand over my hair. "I know, darling." He leaned down and whispered, "And I read his mind. He's going to Potions. No worries."

"Maybe you should go check on him. Take David with you. I want to talk to Will if that's okay. *Not* to have wild sex or anything. I'm taking things with him at a snail's pace." I laughed.

Alder pulled me to my feet and kissed me deeply. I adored the fire in his eyes and wanted to reassure him of my feelings. "I love you, my number one. It might sound like I'm teasing, but you are my forever."

Alder squeezed me tight. "Forever."

My mates left. Harris read my mind and took Trace back to their place and I found Will inside the big walk-in pantry in the café. He stopped chewing a stick of licorice when he saw me. It belonged to Trace. I hated the stuff. I laughed a little at his face. Caught in the act.

"Hungry?" I asked.

"Constantly," he answered.

He swallowed the bite and looked me up and down like I was next on the menu. I pulled my cardigan closed and tore my eyes away from the glinting gold in his.

"Come on, I have mozzarella sticks in David's freezer."

"Score," he said enthusiastically.

I emptied the entire box onto the largest cookie sheet I could find. Will sat on a tall chair at the small island separating the kitchen from the living room.

"Beer and mozz sticks just might be the way to my heart, Willa."

I giggled. "Your stomach, at least."

"Hey, London doesn't have the same kind of bar food you have. I love it."

I set a beer in front of him and sipped my own. "So..."

He gulped down half of his. "So..."

"Will, I want you to know I plan on taking things slow. Yes, we have a bond, but you don't really know that much about me, and you may not even like me after spending some time together."

"You don't really believe that, do you?"

I stared at the amber bottle in my hand. "Not really."

Will took my hand that picked at the frayed knee of my jeans. I knew he felt the energy that flowed out of my palm. He slid his over it.

"This kept me going when I was dying, but without it, I would still be here. I know the reals like to ask for your energy. You are so generous to let them take it. Why do you do it?"

I laced our fingers together. He smiled.

"Well, I guess it's because I have so much. The truth is, if I didn't let it out, I'd go mad. Micah is so good at grounding me. He knows me, probably more than anyone, and when I get full of too many emotions or overwhelmed, he knows. But I really do love giving it to those I trust and care about. I think it would be selfish not to."

"I don't think there's anyone who would accuse you of being selfish."

The oven dinged and I let go of Will's hand. Two more beers and ten mozzarella sticks later, Will smirked when I sat close to him on the couch.

"Don't get too excited," I jokingly warned. "This," I gestured between us with my hand, "really is going to move slowly. I'm not jumping into it head first."

Will put his arm around me and I curled up on his warm chest. His stomach growled.

"Are you still hungry?" I asked.

He laughed. "Yes. Will you go to the bar down the street with me? They have great greasy food."

I hopped up. "Sounds delicious."

DAVID

After two bottles of warm blood, Micah still sat sulking with resting bitch face. Alder raised his eyebrows at me.

"What do you think they're doing?" Micah scowled.

"I'm sure Willa's talking and Will's probably eating," I joked, trying to lighten the mood.

Micah huffed and rolled his eyes. "Animal."

"Micah," Alder scolded him.

"Will can't control who he bonds with, you know," I said. "How do you think I feel? He's my protector."

"How *do* you feel? Cause it doesn't seem to bother the two of you one bit," he complained to me and Alder.

Alder spoke up with a tone of sincerity and authority. "Micah, I knew Willa was my mate long before I met her. Then you were there. Unexpectedly, I felt a fated connection there too. But what if I had rejected you? I had the power to do so. I learned years ago to graciously receive what the universe offers. I'm no god. None of us are. We're in a bloody chaotic world and I think it's wise to gather all the love we can. Hold on to it and let that love multiply. You know Willa has so much to give and we have all saved one another in some form or fashion."

Micah showed his emotions in front of me and Alder before when Alder spoke about Willa in my office at Lust. Tears rolled down Micah's face again now and he wiped them away and smiled. He and Alder stood and embraced.

"I love you," Micah whispered into Alder's ear.

They sat back down.

"I'm sorry. I'm great at helping Willa ground, but I think I need a good grounding myself," Micah admitted.

"David and Will are going back to London for a little while. Harris and I are going to go with them. We'll be delivering Levi to Castle Blair, then Harris and I will return. You'll get some quality time with Willa for a couple of days." Alder smiled.

Micah sighed. "Thank you. Sorry, I'm so needy."

I patted his knee. "I get it. And thanks for putting up with me. I feel accepted and it means the world to me."

WILLA

The bar had great vibes and Will wasn't lying about the food. We both devoured smash burgers with all the fixings and hand cut fries.

"See? Perfect, innit?"

I wiped my greasy fingers on a napkin. "God, yes. So good. I'm so glad this place is within walking distance. Not that I need it to be so readily available," I laughed.

"So, I'm drunk and I have a confession." Will leaned in close.

I laughed. "What?"

"I shagged a girl in the loo the last time I was here."

His face looked concerned that I would be upset. He chewed his thumbnail and waited for my response.

"Will. God, lighten up. She's not here now, is she? She doesn't work here or something, does she?"

"Fuck no. She was with her sister's bachelorette party from Tennessee. Very sweet lass and I did *not* take advantage of her. She had her way with me," he added with emphasis.

"Ha! I bet she *was* sweet," I joked.

His face looked relieved. "Thanks for not holding it against me."

"Is your libido wolf like?" I was genuinely curious.

"Mmm, well...yes."

I took a long sip of my beer not knowing how to respond. Thinking about sex with Will made my body vibrate and I had to shut the thoughts out for the time being. I was seriously not rushing anything with him. Micah and his feelings were too important, and I knew that relationship needed nurturing first. I had faith everything would work out in its own time.

I raised my bottle. "Here's to new friendships with benefits, in the future, down the road," I joked.

Will clinked his beer against mine with the familiar golden flicker in his eyes.

We walked back hand in hand and entered the courtyard. I stopped and pulled Will back from David's door. He looked confused.

"Wait," I said quietly. "I think we just went on our first date."

His face beamed. "Yes, I guess we did."

I pulled him closer. I wrapped his arms around me, and he rested his chin on the top of my head. He was a little taller than Alder and David, like Micah.

After a minute, I leaned back. "I had a great time. Thanks for getting me out of the house."

Will moved in, but only kissed my forehead. "Best first date ever."

"I'm going to say goodnight to Alder and Micah. Tell David I'll be back in a minute."

Micah opened the door before I could knock and tugged me against himself.

"I'm so sorry, Willa. Please don't be mad at me. I had a moment of insanity."

"Micah, ease up. You're suffocating me."

We laughed and I heard Alder's voice.

"Well, let her in."

He let go but kept a hand on the small of my back.

"It's okay to have feelings. Strong ones. I would be upset if you were indifferent. I had to check on you and tell you both goodnight."

Alder kissed my mouth and then playfully placed little kisses down my neck. "We love you, darling. Sleep well."

I gave Micah a long kiss and left. David leaned against his door, waiting for me across the courtyard.

"Had to make sure you got home okay," he said with a smolder when I reached him.

"In the mood to go riding before sun up," I teasingly asked.

David threw me over his shoulder and had me inside and into his bed within seconds.

Eighteen

WILLA

It had been a couple of days and nights without drama, but almost everyone would be leaving soon to take Levi to Castle Blair and David and Will planned on staying in London for about a month. I spent most of my time with David while I could. Micah would be staying with me and Trace when they were gone. Alder and Harris promised they would return within two nights.

I sat alone at the long coffee bar. I woke before sunset and everyone else as I often did. The quiet moments, other than outside street noises, calmed me and allowed time to have a cup of coffee by myself. I often recited meditative or manifesting mantras as I stirred in the creamer. Trace joined me after a little while and I handed her a full mug the way she always took it.

"Are you as nervous about them going to Castle Blair as I am?" she asked me.

"I'm sure the vampires can handle it. David said Alder was quite cruel with Rafe. I can hardly imagine it. Alder is usually so calm and even tempered. Even with Cateline and Wesley he seemed to just do what had to be done along with the others, but David said he was tortuous with Rafe."

I shuddered at the thought.

"Alder is kind, but he will fiercely defend you and everyone he loves. I'm thankful to be on his good side," she joked. "Hey, you get to spend some quality time with Micah, and we can keep busy around here."

After Dark wouldn't open for a couple of months, and Trace and I wanted to set our intentions clearly and completely. Attract good energy, success, and wellbeing while repelling negativity. Marita offered a lot of advice on the subject and Trace ordered various plants and crystals to place around the space.

When the sun went down, the vampires emerged along with Will who slid onto the high stool next to me.

"Who wants take-out?" he asked.

"Everyone, I'm sure," I answered.

"You better get your fill tonight. We leave well before dawn to arrive at Castle Blair after dark. We can take along some snacks, but still," Alder said.

"I wish you could take me along as a snack," I teased. The light in Alder's eyes flashed.

"Hey, you're staying right here with me," Micah said with a sexy smirk. I blushed thinking about how much I wanted to assure him he would never be replaced, but first I needed to give Alder and David something for the trip. "I'll be back shortly," I told him.

The two of them read my mind and followed me up the staircase to Alder and Micah's place. As soon as the door closed behind us, hands roamed my body. Alder's mouth found my neck and David groaned when Alder's fangs sank into my flesh. Alder's hands squeezed my ass and David held my hips while guiding me down onto the sofa. Alder continued to drink. David tilted my head back further while Alder kept going and I whispered, "Come, take me at the same time."

David leaned in and bit down below my earlobe. The sucking sounds, hot wet lips, and sharp fangs had my body tingling. Their tongues swept over the wounds and then we thoroughly enjoyed kissing each other. Both of them tasted like my blood.

"I love you both so much. Please take care of each other while you're gone," I said.

"I promise, darling. Thank you for giving us a taste. I'll think about you every minute I'm away. I'm going back down to give you two a few minutes alone," Alder said.

David ran a hand under my hair and massaged the back of my head. "Mmm, I'm going to miss you, babe."

We kissed some more, and I curled up as close as I could on his chest. "I'll project to you after you've been back in London a few nights. I love you, my wild one."

WILL

I smelled Willa's scent on Alder. He sat beside me while I ate two orders of kung pao chicken.

"Are you ready to see your brother?" he asked, sincerely concerned.

"I am. I've had time to get over the initial fury over what he did, and a not so civil confrontation may be in order, but I don't want to show him any emotion. I refuse to give Levi any more of my energy. I think I learned that from Willa. Watching her and the way she is so intentional with herself, her energy, and her soul, has made me want to be a better man. I mean, more well-rounded, I guess. Guarding myself and others while giving what I can. Am I making any sense?" I asked as I laughed at my ramblings.

"More than you think, mate. And aren't we all better off for it? I knew what I was missing before Willa and I finally came together, but not *really*. Nothing compares to the privilege of having her, holding her..." Alder shook his head. He snapped out of his thoughts when Willa and David walked down the steps hand in hand, and I saw a glow of adoration in Alder's eyes as he watched them.

"I went on and on, didn't I," Alder admitted.

"I'm beginning to understand."

David kissed Willa's forehead before letting her go and she came my way. She put her hands on my shoulders and leaned over, smelling the food.

"Mmm, looks delicious. I'll have some in a minute, but will you walk outside with me for a second?"

I jumped up so fast. Too eager. We stood on the front porch

and watched people milling around for a minute. I had come to love New Orleans. Willa slid an arm through mine and clutched my bicep. I felt peaceful and loving energy flowing from her palm. I absorbed all I could get. I looked down at her and we studied each other for a moment without speaking.

"Your dark eyes glint with a beautiful gold when you look at me. I love it," she said quietly and sweetly. "I had to tell you that I'm sorry for what you went through while you were here."

When I opened my mouth to speak, she stopped me. "Will, wait. I'm serious. Half of us were practically strangers to you, but you trusted us in your most desperate time. I keep thinking back on it. I may sound silly, but I hope I didn't make you feel like you weren't wanted or say anything horrible while you couldn't communicate with us. I was tired and frustrated and confused about the whole situation, and I didn't know you were the poor wolf."

I had to stop her. I put my hand over her mouth. Her eyes went wide with surprise.

"Stop, woman. Just stop." I felt her mouth curve up under my palm and reluctantly took away my hand. The scenario of kissing her hard right there in the moment flashed through my mind. Oh, she would be worth the wait. I took both of her hands and held them to my chest. "Willa, you and Trace saved me. Well, and David's vampire blood," I joked, "but you and I had a bond and that gave me a reason to survive."

I pulled one of her hands up to my ear and made her caress it. "And this."

She realized what I was referring to. Her fingers began rubbing my earlobe. I hummed and closed my eyes.

"Yes, Willa. Do you realize what this simple gesture meant to me? Do you even remember doing this?"

She went onto her tiptoes and gently kissed my cheek. "I remember," she whispered into my ear.

I wrapped her up in my arms and she pressed her cheek to my heart and mumbled into my chest.

"It was the only place that wasn't hurt. I wanted you to know I was there, and I wanted you to feel my touch, even if I did think you were just a wolf."

"I did. I did, love."

Nineteen

WILLA

Micah easily said goodbye to Alder, Harris, David, and Will. He was ready to have me all to himself, but my heart ached a little watching them leave.

He grabbed onto me from behind as soon as the black SUV pulled away, dragging me backwards and kissing my neck with every step.

"Oh, lord, you two. I think I'll go back to my place," Trace said, rolling her eyes.

"No. Wait," Micah offered with thick sarcasm as she left, waving his words away. He sat on the piano bench with his back to the keys and me on his lap. His hard on pressed against the back of my thigh.

"I should learn to play this thing. It turns you on when Alder or David play. I can tell."

I moved my hips in a slow seductive circle, rubbing his cock, and he hissed. "Shit."

His fingers dug into my hips, and he pushed them down. "You have started a fire in me that will not die. I want to ruin you, Willa. Slowly."

Fuck. I would let Micah do anything he wanted to me. His

hands found my breasts and squeezed, and I begged, "Take me upstairs, please."

He pushed me up from his lap and I walked ahead of him. I almost tripped up the steps when Micah slid his hand between my legs and fingered me over my leggings. I panted and he kept his hand there, torturing me in the best way, until we made our way through the apartment and to the bed. I didn't turn around but bent over the mattress and kept his hand in place with my own.

"Oh, Willa, not yet," he said when he pulled away.

Damn, that's what I told David when we were at Lust in his playroom. Now I was on the receiving end, and I admittedly liked it. Micah turned me around to face him and undressed me. I would never tire of looking at his face. His eyes glowed and his fangs descended. He shoved me backwards onto the bed with force and I laughed with excited anticipation when I bounced on the mattress, then he slowly stripped, wearing only a wicked grin. Micah's body looked as though it was carved by Michelangelo. He crawled on all fours and hovered above me. We both savored this precious time together. I wanted to touch him badly, so I reached down and stroked his cock with my vibrating hand. He made no protest. Micah wrapped a hand around my throat and tilted up my chin with his thumb. His wet tongue swiped across the spot where Alder had bitten me under my ear, but he only kissed it. I stroked him a few more times before he moved to switch positions. I grabbed his hand and shoved his index and middle fingers into my mouth, sucking hard and twirling my tongue around them. He gasped.

"Fuck, Willa, you want it in your mouth, don't you? You want me to fuck that pretty mouth?"

I nodded and my body writhed at the thought. I slithered down to where he was on his knees and turned so that Micah could have full access. He slid it past my lips slowly and after he knew I could take it, he pumped his cock in and out of my mouth fast and hard. I was surprised when he pulled out after just a couple of minutes but didn't have time to think. Micah flipped me over onto my knees, thrusted his cock into my throbbing pussy, and took me from behind. His fingers pleasured my clit while he pounded into me, and we both tumbled over the edge of ecstasy. He panted with his body bent over mine and his forehead on my back. His blond curls tickled my skin, and a secure arm held me up around my waist. I thought he would probably want a shower and some rest, but he turned me over and rubbed a palm from my collarbone, over my breast, then down my side to my waist. Micah moved lower and locked his arms under my legs, licking a sensitive spot of my inner thigh. His fangs sank in, and I ran my hands through his hair while he satiated his thirst.

It had been a long time since I woke up with only Micah in my bed. Watching his sleeping face brought me peace. Micah's soul never failed to calm my own and now I couldn't imagine life without him. His life had been threatened twice before and it was almost my undoing. My powers as a witch had helped, but the vampires were much stronger. My own physical weakness was a big reason I wanted to be turned. So that me, Micah, and everyone else I loved wouldn't be so vulnerable. I often felt like a liability.

"You're being too hard on yourself and selling yourself short," Micah whispered. He opened his sleepy eyes and smiled. "I was playing opossum."

I poked his ribs. "You cheater. I seriously wish I could block you from reading my mind, damnit."

Micah pulled me close. "Do we have to get up?"

I reached over and looked at my phone. 6 p.m.

"I guess not. Let's cuddle for a while. Trace and I want to walk around the neighborhood to check it out before it gets too late though. We haven't had the chance to. Marita is meeting us here around seven and you're going with us."

"Of course I am. I'm not letting you out of my sight."

DAVID

Hell. The name given to the lowest level of Castle Blair was fitting. When you think of a centuries-old prison, one usually imagines a dungeon with dank, filthy cells and rusty chains bolted to the walls, but the word dungeon didn't do this place justice. No, Hell was all of that and more. More deathly stink, torture devices in eternal use, and never-ending screams of anguish. Usually, no one who entered ever left. Rafe had escaped with help from the inside, and I now stood in front of the tiny room that held the low life who aided him. The traitor was a vampire. The most pitiful vampire I had ever seen. His body was thin and gray, and blood had run from his mouth, covering his chin, and dripped down his chest resembling melted candle wax. One fang showed when he called out for mercy. I winced and gagged when I noticed his other fang was missing along with most of his other teeth. The hulk of a man who delivered the vampire's punishment held a bloody pair of pliers. He slung them downward and released a molar, dropping it into a metal pan with a cringeworthy clink.

"He's a shifter," Will whispered. "This life could have been my fate."

I swung around to look at him. "What? Why?"

"It's maddening for shifters who either can't have the one they bond with or never find a mate. Sure, they can go on, trying to live a normal life, but as the years go by, it eats at them. Depression and anger can build and build until they need an outlet. This is the perfect place to become and act out what they feel they are."

"And what's that?" I asked, unsure if I wanted to hear the answer.

"Unworthy. Unworthy of love or peace or happiness."

Alder squeezed Will's shoulder. "But this isn't your fate, mate."

I grabbed onto Will's hand and held it while we made our way to Levi's cell. Levi sat on the dirt floor naked. He rocked back and forth with a distant look on his face, and Will turned away when he saw him.

"I don't think I can do this. I don't want to be here." He squeezed his eyes shut and I held his face in my hands. I could see he was about to break.

"Will?"

He opened his eyes. "Yes, boss?"

"I've got you. I'm getting you out of here, okay? Do you understand?"

He nodded and we got the fuck out of Hell.

WILLA

We enjoyed the live jazz music as we walked along Frenchmen Street and made a loop through Washington Square before continuing north. Marita acted as our tour guide and Trace had her phone out, searching the map for any places we might want to check out. Micah and I followed hand in hand, not really paying attention to anything they said. We were content enjoying the night air and each other's company.

"Oh, ooo! A Walgreens! Just up ahead on the right. I need to run in for a few necessities," Trace exclaimed.

I perked up. "Oh, me too."

We reached the intersection and waited behind a large group for the light to halt traffic. The bright white WALK sign lit up and a couple of cyclists zoomed past as we joined the back of the herd. Marita and Trace were the stragglers. As soon as my feet hit the sidewalk on the other side, I heard a car horn and screeching brakes. Gasps and screams followed. Micah covered my body with his own and shoved us down. I expected to hear gun shots next, not Marita yelling, "Call 9-1-1."

"Wait, what," I said, crawling out from under Micah.

I glanced around. People stood in a circle around Marita who hunched over Trace. My best friend had been hit by a speeding car that ran the red light. My body froze and vibrated. It felt like I was about to astral project. I guessed it was like a flight or fight response to the extreme situation I found myself in. I had to force myself to stay. Marita looked up and reached out for me. Micah put his hands on my shoulders, bringing me out of the stationary state. He pushed me towards Trace and shock took over my entire being. It was very apparent that either the car or the ground had caused trauma to both her head and chest. I couldn't tell. Blood saturated her purple t-shirt just under her right collarbone and ran from her nose. Micah's eyes were wild as he assessed her. Trace was unresponsive.

"I can't do CPR. She's losing too much blood from her chest. She's not breathing," he exclaimed. "Come here." He pulled me near and spoke low. "She can't leave in an ambulance."

"Wait. Why?"

"If she dies on the way to the hospital or *at* the hospital, I won't be able to turn her."

"He's right," Marita stated.

"Oh fuck," I whispered with ringing in my ears.

They were right. If Trace went to the emergency room, she would be whisked away, and her fate would be in the doctor's hands. With a dying pulse and so much blood loss, Micah making her immortal was the only option. I began to weep, overwhelmed with the situation. Marita nodded to Micah. He scooped her up and was gone in an instant. Marita grabbed my arm and pulled me away from the crowd. Thank goodness, the police hadn't shown up yet.

"Let's go," Marita ordered. "You'll call Alder as soon as we get home. Surely, he and Harris can talk Micah through this."

Twenty

WILLA

We ran so fast and flew into the coffee shop. Micah held Trace tight against his chest and I ran upstairs and yanked the comforter off my bed. I threw it down at the bottom of the stairs so Micah could lay Trace down and I pulled out my phone.

"Alder! Get Harris and put me on speaker. Now!"

"What's happened to Trace?" Harris asked. "Something's wrong. I feel it."

I clicked mine on speaker and Micah explained.

"A car. She was hit by a car. I have to turn her. Like, now."

"No," Harris screamed.

"Brother! If he must, he must," Alder told Harris firmly.

Harris sniffled and began to cry. Alder stepped up and took control. His voice was confident through the phone. "You're going to have to drink her blood. Whatever she has left. Remember your training? Listen to the beat of her heart. Feel the pulse and how it slows against your lips."

Micah placed her limp body in his lap, leaned down, and bit her neck. He sucked a few times then stopped and looked at me.

"She's almost gone." Tears filled his eyes and mine, but we

knew this wasn't the end. I reached to hold her cold hand, giving her any energy I could, and Micah placed his lips to the wound again. Marita chanted words I couldn't understand. Micah took the last of her and sat up.

"That's it. That's all," he spoke to Alder.

"Bite your wrist and give her what she needs," Alder said quietly.

It seemed like time stood still for the first moments after Micah held his wrist to Trace's lips. She was lifeless, but then...

"Oh my god." Micah smiled, and his shoulders relaxed when Trace took her first sip. A tear rolled down his cheek.

"Is she feeding?" Harris pressed.

"Yes, yes," I laughed. Peace washed over all of us as Trace drank Micah's eternal life-giving vampire blood. Marita and I watched in amazement.

"Fuck me," Harris said in relief.

"Well done, Micah," Alder praised. "Well done."

"How much should I let her take?" Micah asked.

"If Trace is drinking on her own, it's enough. It doesn't take much," Harris answered. He laughed again. "Oh my god, she's okay. She's fucking okay. Thank you, Micah. Thank you."

"You're welcome, but you're going to have to tell me what comes next."

"Yes, what now?" I asked.

Trace's eyelids fluttered but remained closed. She turned towards Micah's chest, and he gathered her close.

"Now you have to make sure she feels safe when she wakes and...Willa, she will need to feed and I don't want it to be from you," Alder said firmly.

"Okay, I'm sure I can find a real who would be willing if I promise to give them some of my energy in return."

Marita spoke up. "Alder, I will stick around. I'm here for the duration. I'll make sure Willa stays safe too."

"I don't want to get off of the phone with you two, but it looks like a massacre happened here," I said as I looked around and my eyes landed on Micah. He had Trace hugged up tight and her blood soaked his shirt. "Micah needs a shower."

"No, I'm not letting her go," he argued.

I was a little taken aback. Oh, shit. Micah drank Trace's blood, and she had his. Micah was her freaking maker. I stammered over my words as anxiety built within. "I...I'll call you in a bit, Alder. We are going to clean up. I love you."

"Harris and I will be back before you know it. We are on our way."

I clicked off my phone and the room went silent. I clammed up, not knowing what the fuck all of this meant. "You do whatever, but you need a shower and Trace probably needs to be in a bed, so she's comfortable."

Marita could tell I was off. "Come." She took me into the half bath under the staircase. She lathered up her hands and forearms and handed me the soap. "Don't panic, Willa. Take a few deep breaths and try not to say anything out of jealousy."

I looked at her, hurt over her words, but I was jealous.

"I feel you. You know I'm an empath. And it's practically shooting out of your eyes like daggers."

I only sighed.

We dried our hands and Marita brushed my hair behind my ears. "Time to face the unknown again, but we're getting pretty good at getting through it, aren't we?"

She made me smile a little even though the sinking feeling remained. "We are." I did as she suggested and took deep breaths. "Okay, will you help me pry Trace out of Micah's arms and get her into a bed?"

Micah rocked Trace like a baby and when our eyes met, his looked apologetic. I knelt beside them. "Don't you think she needs to be wrapped up, comfy in a bed? Take her up to mine. Marita and I can watch her while you get cleaned up."

He started to protest, but I hushed him. "You can jump in my shower, right there near her. I promise, I'll get you out if she stirs. Marita and I won't leave her until you are finished and back by her side."

He looked down at Trace then back at me. He loosened his hold only slightly. I gently touched his face. "I promise."

Micah adjusted her position and carried her upstairs to my bed.

We tucked her in, and I pushed him toward the bathroom. "I'll bring you a change of clothes."

I shut the door, leaned on it, and shook my head at Marita who sat next to Trace. Whenever I found myself in a situation I didn't know how to handle, it felt like a fog settled over me. All of my movements were mechanical; like I was just going through the motions. My tired mind knew morning would come soon.

I put Micah's clothes by the sink and sat on the toilet. "Are you okay?"

"I don't know. Would you be okay? I won't have that answer until I know Trace is okay."

God, he was so serious. I wanted Trace to be fine. Fuck, she would be fine. She was a damn vampire now. And I wasn't. It stung. All I wanted to do was go back in time. I should have stayed in bed with Micah until Alder had returned from his trip. Then, none of this would've happened. I wanted to get naked, step into the shower with him, and forget all about it for a few minutes. I wanted to press myself against Micah's tall body with his arms wrapped around me and slip my tongue into his mouth, so we could consume each other and feel the togetherness we had only hours ago. I stood and put my hand on the door knob. I hesitated, but left Micah alone.

I laid on the floor at Marita's feet.

"I need Alder," I cried. "I wish he was here."

"He'll be back soon. You know he and Harris can't wait for the sun to go down. Harris is going to have to deal with all of this too. You know he wanted to be the one to turn her."

I huffed. "I know. I'm trying my hardest not to curse the universe right now."

Micah came out of the bathroom, and I sat up and quickly wiped away the tears. Wet blond curls fell over his forehead, and he slicked them back. He looked at Trace then to me. He didn't come to me. Instead, he laid across the foot of my bed. Trace didn't move. Marita pulled a blanket around herself and slept in the chair beside the bed, and I locked myself in the bathroom to have another cry.

My phone rang and I was super surprised to see Will's name on the screen.

"Hey," I said.

"Willa, I heard what happened. How are you, love?"

I sniffled. "Well, not great," I admitted.

"I wish I was there to hold your hand. And I know David would if he could. He hates that he had just left town when all of this went down."

"I know. Who would've known. Such a fucking curve ball."

"Oh, shit. I didn't realize what time it is. I should be letting you get some sleep."

At least *someone* cared about how I was feeling.

"No, I...I want to talk to you. I'm having a hard time. Micah has flipped a switch. This maker thing is going to be a huge deal, isn't it?"

Will sighed. "I mean, maybe. Yes, probably."

"Micah will barely look at me. I can't wait for Alder to get here. I'm all twisted up inside."

"I'm sending you the biggest tightest hug through the phone right now. You feel it?"

That made me smile and feel the tiniest butterfly in my stomach. "I feel it."

"And when the smoke clears, Micah's gonna feel like a wanker for ignoring your feelings through all of this. Believe me, he'll be back in your arms soon enough."

"I hope so. And Will? Thank you for being here and being you."

"You're welcome, love. Go get some rest."

Twenty-One

WILLA

T startled awake to the sound of Alder's booming voice on the other side of the bathroom door. My body was stiff and sore from falling asleep leaned against the wall.

"What the fuck? You left Willa alone? To sleep in a bathroom," Alder yelled at Micah I presumed.

He banged on the door, and I reached up to unlock it. He burst in, scooped me up, and held me against his chest. I latched on so hard and sobbed. He rubbed my hair.

"I'm sorry. I'm so sorry I wasn't here, darling," Alder soothed me. "Everything's going to be okay. We always figure things out."

I leaned back and kissed him. "I needed you."

He kissed me back. "I'm here now. I'm so frustrated right now, but it will clear. And Micah can't help it. Please know, he has no control over the powerful pull that exists between him and Trace. Harris and I had to have a real heart to heart about all of it on our way home. That being said, he shouldn't have left you in here alone."

"How is Trace? Is she awake?"

Alder sat me on my feet but didn't let go. "She's awake and feeding from Marita. The shop is still a mess, so they are down there. Marita has a friend coming over later so Trace won't get hungry. Harris and Micah are with them to teach Trace how to do it. There are rules that help." Alder held my face in his hands. "She asked about you. Asked where you were and began profusely apologizing."

"Apologizing for what?"

"For Micah being the one who turned her."

My heart hurt. Of course Trace would apologize for something out of her control especially knowing Harris lost his chance to be her maker. And now it could never be undone. I wanted to speak to her and have a talk with Micah. "Let's go down. I need coffee with a quickness."

I paused at the bottom of the steps. Trace wiped her mouth and Marita sat up straight. "You did so well," she told Trace with a smile.

Her eyes landed on me. Her green eyes that now displayed the vampire glow beautifully. She jumped up.

"Willa!"

"Hey, bestie," I said meekly. She ran over and hugged me.

"Willa, I have so much to say to you, but first I have to thank you for saving me."

"What? I didn't save you. I don't understand." I looked around at everyone.

Trace held both of my hands. Hers weren't as warm as mine now, but the energy in her fingertips vibrated like crazy. "You let Micah turn me. If you had protested in any way...I mean, if I'm being honest, I'm grieving the fact that Harris wasn't the one who..." She continued through tears, "I know the thought of Micah being my maker had to be a shock. If you would have said no, he wouldn't have done it."

Micah looked at the floor. "It's true and I'm sorry for having to make that decision in a moment of such trauma."

His eyes stayed trained on his bare feet. I hugged Trace again. "I could never ever let you die. No matter what. And you would have."

"I know it had to be done and I'm glad you didn't protest," Harris said. "But it still hurts and that's a normal reaction."

Trace went to him, and he pulled her onto his lap. I needed a few moments to myself and went to make coffee. Alder read my mind and left me alone. I drank it too fast and burned my tongue. It sent my frustration through the roof.

"Owww, fuck! Fuck me."

Alder was next to me in an instant. He took the mug from me and set it down, then pulled me in for a kiss. His tongue played with mine and the stinging faded until it felt normal. I didn't know he could do that, although I should have. He always licked the wound he made when he drank from me and it healed so fast. He pulled back a little.

"Better?"

"Mmm, yes. Thank you," I hummed. He leaned and whispered "mine" into my ear. Alder's simple act of care and concern eased my mind and calmed my spirit.

"So, when's it my turn?"

"For what?" Alder asked, knowing exactly what I meant.

I replied to Alder only in my thoughts. I didn't want to speak them aloud. "It can't happen like this for me. I don't want an emergency to make it necessary and I want it to be you. I want *you* to make me immortal. No one else. Do you understand?"

A flickering fire lit in Alder's eyes. He understood. The seriousness of my words hit home. Anyone else turning me wasn't an option for us. It just wasn't. Deep down, he knew I was forcing his hand and he realized I had a valid stance on this. Our bond would never be the same if Alder wasn't my maker and neither he or I could live like that for eternity.

Micah's voice made me nearly jump out of my skin. "Willa," he held out his hand, "can I?"

He pulled me into a hug, and I smelled my shower gel on him. He tightened his arm around my waist and one hand moved up to the back of my head. He massaged my scalp. "Damn, Willa. I'm sorry."

"Tell him how you feel," Alder said to me.

I led Micah to the little bathroom under the stairs and I hopped up onto the vanity.

"Thank you for apologizing. I felt like you had forgotten all about me and I needed you to say it, but from here on out, you're forgiven."

He stepped in between my knees, and I ran my hands through his blonde wavy hair. "Remember the first time we made out at the Glass Animals concert?"

He chuckled and grinned. "Oh yeah."

I sent positive energy through my fingertips. "And the night Alder asked you to move in with me and be our mate?"

Micah blushed and gave me a soft kiss on the cheek. "Mmm hmm."

"Do you remember two nights ago when you were so excited to have me all to yourself?"

He grabbed my ass, slid me as close as our bodies could get, and had his way with my neck between words. "Yes...Willa...I definitely...remember...that."

I gasped at the sensation of his mouth on my sensitive skin and fangs scraping under my jaw line. "Take a drink, Micah. Remember the way I taste."

He growled and sank into me.

MICAH

It didn't take much of Willa's blood to bring me to my senses. No, I couldn't deny the new connection to Trace, and being her maker should have put that connection on a higher level, but the universe wouldn't allow it. Tasting my Willa reaffirmed her place in my world. Trace had been like a sister to me, and our bond would remain that way with the added need to make sure she was protected. Even after I turned her and had tunnel vision during it all, it never felt sexual. The thought made me cringe now. I hated that Willa worried about that.

Trace was on the couch with Marita's friend when Willa and I came out of the bathroom. It was strange watching Trace feed. Willa paused and I read her thoughts. She wondered if she was ready for all of it. I guided her to the bar with my hands securely on her shoulders.

"You need to eat, my little human."

Her stomach growled. "Oh, yeah. Marita and her friend might want something too. We're the only humans here," she scoffed.

Just then someone I recognized came into the shop holding takeout bags. Belle, one of the twins Willa and I had been acquaintances with a while back. My eyes darted to the couch where Trace was feeding. There sat Violet, Belle's twin, with her eyes closed, thoroughly enjoying giving a donation.

"Oh, Belle. Hi," Willa hesitated in her greeting.

"Hey, you two," she said to me and Willa in her sweet southern drawl. "I brought po' boys and all the sides you can eat. I figured us humans might be hungry."

She took out box after box and Willa accepted it happily. Her face was still confused, but she appreciated the gesture. Willa looked at me and I read her mind.

"Whatever, I guess. I can't believe anything surprises me anymore."

I laughed and plucked a french fry from Willa's plate before serving up Vena to the vampires. Alder clinked his glass to mine. He knew Willa and I had made up, reconnected, and were both working through our feelings.

"Cheers, mate," he said in a husky voice with a sexy wink. We went to sit with Willa while she ate, and I continued to graze from her plate.

Trace finished feeding and Violet skipped over to join us. Willa said hello then showed her true colors of kindness and understanding.

"Thank you both for being here. We all appreciate your generosity. I would be happy to sit with each of you and give you some energy for a little while to return the favor," she said.

"Oh, that would be so nice," Violet replied.

"And we don't want much, Willa. It's exciting and energizing just being here with all of you." Belle beamed.

"Still, you deserve it," Willa added. "Especially if you plan on being regulars."

The twins giggled and love for Willa washed through me, watching the way she handled the whole situation. Anyone else probably would have run for the hills, but not Willa.

Twenty-Two

WILLA

I took Belle to Trace's tarot table in the other room while Violet finished her food and chatted with Alder and Micah. I had to admit, after the surprise of seeing the twins, I was more than okay with having familiar faces around. I didn't like the idea of finding random reals from the vampire bars around town to offer their services.

My energy cycled out after giving some to Violet and Belle. I sat at the tarot table alone for a few minutes before Trace walked through the beaded curtain. She looked gorgeous. Her skin glowed and her eyes shimmered with silver sparkles. She sat across from me and we held each other's hands.

"I told you I'd be the guinea pig," Trace joked.

"Trace, I don't ever want you to think that I'm mad at you. These are the cards the universe dealt us."

She laughed. "Is that supposed to be a play on words since we are sitting here in my tarot parlor?"

"No, but it works, right?"

Trace sighed. "Look at us. Look at this place and how things have changed. I still think of Micah as a little brother, you know. There's no way in hell our relationship could be anything else."

I was happy to hear that Trace had that safe mental block where nothing sexual would ever happen between my best friends.

"You should call him daddy just to fuck with him," I teased.

She busted out laughing. "Willa, shut up!"

The others looked our way from the other room.

"It would be hilarious though," she joked. "I might."

"I told Alder I'm ready. I want it to happen soon," I blurted out.

Trace's smile went away. "I get it. I think it's time, too. Alder should be your maker. You shouldn't wait until something crazy happens and your choice is taken away."

"Exactly! I explained it to him in that context and he understands completely. I want it to be planned and I haven't told Alder, but I want everyone together. David and Will, too. Do you think that's silly?"

"Hell, no. We should make it an event. Why not? I could ask Harris to take me to London for some training. Everyone would conveniently be present."

"I like the way you think, bestie." I smiled.

Trace touched her abdomen. "I'm feeling the pain again and I hear your heartbeat like my ear is to your chest. Think it's Belle's turn. The sun will be up in a little bit."

WILLA

Nothing compared to being snuggled in between Alder and Micah and I had slept like a baby. We only rested because the past two nights had been so chaotic. No sex, but both were pressed as close as possible. Their arms and legs were touching each other's across my body. I loved it. I had my own nest made of vampire bodies. I laughed at myself, and Micah mumbled into my ear from behind.

"There you go being a comedian again."

"I refuse to elbow you again since your abs practically cracked my olecranon last time."

"What the fuck is that?"

"It's the pointy bone that you feel when you bend your arm at the elbow. I thought everyone new that."

"Ha ha, smarty pants. Did you know that fun fact, Alder?"

"Yes," Alder answered confidently.

"Pshhh," Micah hissed as he started kissing my shoulder. "You two don't want me for my brain. You want me for my body."

Alder and I laughed, and I squirmed against Micah's hard cock. Alder opened his eyes and winked.

"I would fancy seeing both of your bodies in the shower in five," Alder suggested before getting out of bed and sauntering naked into the bathroom. Micah and I trailed close behind.

We had a thoroughly good time and a thorough washing before heading down to the shop. I wanted to check on Trace. She had Harris to take care of her, but she was my best friend, and after the shock of it all, I was kind of obsessed with the idea of her as a true vampire.

She and Harris sat on stools at the bar drinking Vena. I smelled coffee brewing. Trace had started it for me and any other humans who might stop in. I fully expected Marita, Belle, and Violet to return. I hugged her from behind.

"Thanks for thinking of me."

"I know how you get without it," Trace spoke truthfully.

"Wise woman," Micah said.

"Yeah, yeah. Bitch before coffee," I admitted.

"Willa," Alder warned. He hated that word and hated me calling myself a bitch even if I was joking. I wrapped around him, and he held on. "You love me without coffee, don't you?"

"Of course, darling."

I kissed his cheek and let go to add sugar and creamer to my mug.

"It will be strange not needing it after I'm turned. I bet I'll still crave it. It's ingrained in me." I laughed.

No one else laughed. They all stared at me.

"What? Stop being so serious. It's happening and you all may as well accept it."

"Do you know Trace and Willa have been scheming?" Harris asked Alder.

I gulped nervously. Trace winced. Alder's eyes darted back and forth between us.

"Out with it," he demanded.

We both sat silent.

"I'm not angry. Tell me what this big plan is," Alder softened and resigned himself to the fact that once Trace and I had a plan, it would be futile to try and stop it.

"Belle and Violet will need a break from me feeding from them soon," Trace stated facts. "I want all of us to take a trip to London. I could train at Lust like Micah, and while we're there...Alder can turn Willa surrounded by all of her mates."

She said it beautifully. I swooned. Alder pursed his lips in thought and looked down, tapping his fingers on the countertop. After a few moments of me holding my breath and the room being absolutely silent, he looked up and straight into my eyes. "Okay."

Everyone visibly relaxed because none of us knew how he would respond. His gaze stayed on me, and I wanted him to know how serious I was and how much it meant to me to do it this way, but he knew. He knew me inside and out and when he smiled, I jumped into his arms.

"Why don't you call David and tell him we'll be going on holiday, and he will see you soon. It's about midnight there. He should be around," Alder said.

"Should I mention what all of this is about?"

"Of course. I think he'll be pleased."

WILLA

David and Will were waiting at the airport when the Invictus touched down. Everyone exchanged greetings. I hugged Will tight.

"Long time no see," he joked.

Then I jumped on David, and he swung me around. "Hello, my wild one."

His nose was in my hair, and he kissed behind my ear. "You smell so good, babe. Let's go home."

Two blacked out SUVs took us to David's. We unpacked and convened in the kitchen where Marco cooked Shepard's pie. Excitement pulsated through me, knowing what the next few nights ahead had in store.

We decided it would happen here at David's home. Turning

me in this way wouldn't be messy. Alder promised to make it as peaceful and comfortable as possible.

Twenty-Three

WILL

The house buzzed. Trace gave off more energy now that she was a vampire. Other than that, she hadn't changed all that much. Willa seemed distant. She didn't make eye contact with anyone and picked at her nails. Everyone was getting ready to go to Lust for a night out together, but I saw Alder pull Willa aside. My ears perked up.

"Darling, are you feeling up to it? We don't have to go. No one would mind," he told her.

"I don't want to be the party pooper. I'll manage."

I tentatively stepped over and lightly touched Willa's arm. "Willa, I'm not going, and I would love for you to join me watching old movies or something. Anything you want. We could veg out and do nothing?"

Her face softened and her body visibly relaxed with relief to have an alternative. She looked at Alder and he nodded with a smile. "I think that would be nice. Thank you, Will," he said to me. He kissed her forehead, and I held out my hand to her. It felt like I had my hand wrapped around her beating heart. I squeezed it and she looked at me.

"What is it that you do? Push the energy down through the bottom of your feet?" I asked.

She sighed. "Yes. Maybe we can go sit in David's office for a minute."

I sat close to her on the brown leather sofa. She sat up straight and her bare feet were planted flat on the floor.

"You can do this too, you know. It's like meditating," she suggested.

I straightened myself and flattened my feet. Willa closed her eyes and began deep breathing. I swear I saw a faint glowing in her breastbone.

"Concentrate on the energy inside of you and envision it circling in the center of your chest. When you can see the ball of light in your mind, direct it down slowly until it reaches your feet. Then, all you have to do is push it out and tell it to go. Invite new clean energy in."

It was hard to tear my eyes away from her. Willa was magical. She was strong yet delicate. I finally closed my eyes and did as she instructed. It felt natural. Like it was something I should have been doing all along. No wonder humans went to dark places of sadness, feeling stuck in a rut. They kept the same stale energy swirling within. I understood why the reals wanted to spend time with Willa and Trace. I opened my eyes and looked over at Willa. Her hands glowed with pure light. She knew I was looking, and she turned to me. She held out her palm and I wrapped my fingers around it. She vibrated and I sucked in a breath, feeling like I had been suffocating and Willa resuscitated me.

"We had our first kiss here, David and I," she said wistfully.

I smiled, thinking about my mouth meeting hers.

"That's sweet. You're sweet," I said quietly.

"Thank you for staying home with me. I needed this."

I desperately wanted to confess words of love and adoration, and although they lived in the space between our hearts, I didn't want to be so bold. Willa wanted us to take things slow. Instead, I made her a promise. "When you call, I will come and when you ask me to stay, I will stay."

Willa latched onto me, and I held a precious treasure. I felt her love and I was so thankful to have these moments alone.

"Your eyes were glinting with gold again. I love that," she told me like she had before. I pulled her closer and we leaned back. Her head lay on my chest. She tucked her legs up and I circled a thumb over her kneecap.

"Well, I'll soon be the lone wolf in a house of vampires again."

Willa propped up on my chest to look at me.

"You're just as important as anyone in this house. Don't ever feel less than. You might be *more* important. You're a protector. Sure, vampires are powerful and for the most part immortal, but you're special on a different level. I know David feels that way."

"Thank you for saying so." I blushed. I had felt less than in the past. How could I not? But to be truthful, no one else was responsible for those feelings besides myself.

Willa leaned over and kissed my cheek then said something that made me feel like I could die that night and be happy.

"I am convinced I'm the luckiest girl in the world, but if everything was different, if witches and vampires and shifters didn't exist...if we were regular boring old humans and you and I were sitting in a modest little house in the woods, I would still be the luckiest girl."

I had no words for a moment then got my wits about me. "Is this real life? Pinch me, Willa. I think I'm dreaming."

We laughed and she in fact did pinch me playfully with a squeal.

"Oh no you bloody didn't!"

Willa jumped up and ran down the hall to the living room. I chased after and she let me catch her. We stood pressed together and then she took my breath away again with a kiss. A real, two mouths melting into one, tongues touching, bodies burning kiss. Forget what I said earlier. Now I could die happy. Willa pulled back and we were both out of breath.

"This is monumental," I informed her.

She raised her eyebrows. "Oh, really? Now my head's going to get big."

I led her to sit on the settee with me.

"I'm serious. That was the first time ever kissing my mate."

The realization dawned in her eyes. "Will, I hadn't thought about it that way. You're so right and I'm honored to be yours. I truly am."

I hugged her close again. "Thank you for telling me, my mate."

We both fell asleep around 4 a.m. while watching reruns of Are You Being Served? and I woke to the sound of my stomach growling and everyone else entering the house.

Alder smiled and came to see us, but Micah only glanced our way, then walked on past.

"He's fine," Alder whispered. "Micah will come around."

Willa roused at Alder's voice and stretched when she raised up from my chest.

"Did you two have a nice time?" Alder asked.

"We did. Thanks for trusting me with her," I said.

"My trust in you was never in question, mate. Thank you for taking care of our Willa."

Our Willa. My heart soared at the acceptance offered by Alder. I belonged to this unconventional extraordinary family.

MICAH

Alder, David, Will, and I met in David's office to discuss the turning of Willa. I didn't really like the fact that Will was included, but thankfully he sat quietly while we made plans.

"At first, I selfishly wished it was only Willa and I, but she wants you all to be present, and I understand." Alder stated. He turned to me. "I will turn her. She will drink only my blood, but I want you to drink from Willa with me."

It surprised me that he left David out. Both Alder and David read my mind.

"It's okay. I never dreamed you would all come here to my home and let me be involved in any way with Willa's turning. It means everything to me. I do have one request," David said. "Can I please play the piano for her...during?"

"That's the most beautiful gift you could give her, mate." Alder smiled.

"Can we let it be a surprise?" I asked. "She's going to absolutely love it."

"I'll push the piano into any room you like," David offered.

There was a knock on the door. It was Harris and Trace.

"I have a few ideas, if it's okay with all of you," Trace asked.

"Yes, please Trace. I think you could set the perfect scene."

Twenty-Four

WILLA

Tonight is the night, I thought as soon as I woke up. I slept with David because I knew I would be with Alder and Micah after my turning. I slid from David's bed a little before dawn to take a shower alone. I needed time to gather my thoughts and feelings. I knew I was the only one out of the loop about the plans for the evening, but it excited me. My mates would take care of every detail and I felt giddy thinking about how many people cared and wanted it to be perfect. I hated the way it had happened for Trace, but we had another long talk about it. We both purged any negativity and vowed to move forward with no regrets. I reluctantly shut off the hot water and stepped out of the shower. David had those fancy towel warming stands and the most luxurious Egyptian towels. I wiped the steam from the mirror and peered at myself. This is how I will always look. This will be the eternal me. A sobering thought that should have scared me a little, but it didn't.

David knocked lightly on the door. "Should I come back later?" he asked.

I let him in, and he kissed me.

"Good evening, babe. Big night. Is there anything I can do for you besides make sure hot coffee is ready?"

He made me laugh. "As long as everyone doesn't fawn all over me for the next few hours, I'm all good."

"Noted. Oh, one thing...what's your all-time favorite song, that's not electronic dance music," he laughed.

"Hmm. That's a tough one, but I'll say 'Turning Page' by Sleeping at Last. It makes me feel some sort of way," I answered.

"Perfect." He smiled and kissed the tip of my nose.

Trace found me alone in David's bedroom. He had brought me coffee and told me to stay as long as I like.

"Hey, bestie," I welcomed her in.

She sat next to me and took my hand. "Are you nervous?"

"Not really. More anxious than anything."

"I bet," she said. "I'm excited for you. I know you've been wanting this for a while. And I'm so happy it's going to be Alder. Since all of this began, you and Alder have taught me a lot about the world."

"Really? What do you mean?"

"God, where do I start? The way you love each other, how you share that love, you both have flaws and aren't afraid to show them, and you come out stronger on the other side of anything life throws at you. Harris looks up to Alder more than he knows."

"Trace, promise me we will never leave each other. I know there are so many moving parts, especially in my life, but you and I make up the foundation."

She hugged me tight. "I promise. You know I promise. I have a spell for you, and I'd like to do it with just you and I."

"Let's do it."

Trace took an abalone shell, a lighter, a sweet grass sage stick, tourmaline, and tiger eye stones from her pocket.

"You came prepared," I joked.

I set my coffee mug on the nightstand, and we stood up. Trace lit the sweet grass, placed it in the abalone shell and put it next to my mug. The smoke wafted up between us. She held out her palms. One held tiger eye and the other held tourmaline. I put my hands over hers, feeling the stones between our palms.

Trace recited the spell:

The winds of change I feel within

A new story, peace, and abundance begin
Chapters are closing, new beginnings await
May this new season bring us true love and fate
With this spell
I cast unto thee
I wish all well
So blessed be

We stayed put, meditating, and manifesting as the smell of sweet grass swirled around us.

WILLA

I slipped into the black lace dress I wore the first night Alder and I met. I was in front of a full-length mirror, and he stood behind me, admiring the view. We weren't talking much. The silence of his room held peaceful vibes and Alder took great care in making sure I remained calm. He put his hands on my waist and kissed my bare shoulder.

"Where would you like me to do it?" he asked quietly.

"Why don't you use your favorite spot." I touched my neck just below my ear lobe. He leaned in and put his warm wet mouth on my skin. I tingled all over. "And I think Micah should drink from my wrist. I want to feel his face in my palm."

"Perfect," Alder growled. His fangs had descended in anticipation of what was about to happen.

I turned around to look into his glowing eyes. "My number one. Now and forever."

"Now and forever," he promised.

Alder led me down the hallway and stopped in front of the door to the piano room. It stood open and light from more LED candles than I could count spilled onto the floor in front of my bare feet. A platform bed covered in exquisite bohemian comforters and pillows sat in the middle of the room. A ring of red salt encircled the bed. I could tell Trace had arranged the décor. She knew me so well. Harris and Trace stood inside the doorway. Harris and Alder embraced, and Trace kissed my cheek. Will was knelt down on his knees outside of the salt ring. Micah stood tall and strong behind the bed, waiting for me. Then, the sweetest sound met my ears. David played the first notes of "Turning Page", and I went directly to him. I ran my fingers through the dark curls at the back of his neck and he tilted his head back, acknowledging my presence. I kissed his cheek and rejoined Alder.

He took me to the bed and laid me down. He and Micah were by my side and euphoria settled over me like a blanket.

Micah whispered into my ear. "I love you, Willa."

I touched my palm to his face, and he held it there. He kissed the inside of my wrist where he would be drinking my blood.

Alder ran a thumb over my bottom lip. "Are you ready, my darling?"

I pulled his mouth to my neck. My mates simultaneously sank in their fangs and took all of me. My world went dark.

DAVID

My fingers stopped gliding across the piano keys at the end of the song and I turned to see Micah sit up straight, still holding Willa's wrist. He licked his lips, then licked the wound and left a tender kiss there.

Alder put a hand over her heart and took one final drink. He swiped his tongue over the bite and moved to kiss her on the mouth. Willa lay there lifeless, and I felt jittery inside, waiting for Alder to give her his blood. He lifted her onto his lap, bit into his own wrist, and held it to her lips.

"Take my blood, darling. Take my life. I give you my life. You are my life. We'll be together forever, my mate," he chanted.

Willa licked the drops of his immortal blood from her lips and then consumed more. Alder rocked her like a baby while she drank. We all sighed with relief and Micah caressed Alder's face when he looked at him. Willa drank a good amount, so Alder took his wrist away and wiped her rosy lips. Micah reached for Alder's wrist and licked the wound. The whole event was extraordinary, and I was drawn to them like a magnet. I couldn't stop myself from getting closer. I crawled up near the bed and slowly reached towards Willa. I needed to touch her. Alder was aware of how I felt and turned to me.

"Come, David," he said gruffly, his voice full of emotion.

I tentatively sat on the edge of the bed and Micah placed her hand in mine. I was thankful he allowed me to take part. I pulled it up to my lips. Energy flowed from her fingertips, and I held them to my chest. Alder didn't let go of Willa. Harris and Trace came and placed kisses on her forehead.

"Let me know if you need anything," Trace told Alder and Micah.

"Congratulations, brother," Harris smiled at Alder.

They left and Will remained knelt on the floor with his head down.

"Are you alright, mate," I whispered to him.

He looked at Willa then to me. "I'm not sure. I need to think."

"I know this is a lot," Alder said. "Give her a kiss before you go and take all the time you need to think. We will be here. All of us."

Will came to her and kissed her sweetly on the lips. I grabbed his arm before he turned to leave.

"Don't go far, mate." I was afraid he may run. "Willa will want to see you when she wakes."

Will nodded and I prayed he knew how important he was to Willa and me.

WILL

Well, that was it. The buildup of the emotional night came to an end and my mate had transformed. The reality of it all came crashing down on me like a tidal wave the second Alder drank the last drop of her. It had been a big pill to swallow knowing I bonded with a witch, and I knew Willa would eventually be turned, but it went by so fast, and now I had no clue how to react. I questioned the universe as to why I didn't bond to another wolf shifter. I second guessed my own instincts and intuition and the whole shifter mate bonding practice. Then I kind of shut down. My mind numbed and my soul grieved. Grieved for the human side of Willa. I would eventually get over that, but deep down I was afraid she wouldn't want me anymore. That's why I went numb. It was a defense mechanism. I had shut down before when I had resigned myself to never finding my fated mate. I would live my life as David's protector and shag anyone I wanted and then I would die. Willa had been the one to wake me up from the darkness the night we met. Could I even handle the whole vampire witch thing? Would Willa remember and still feel our bond? Would she still love me?

Acknowledgments

I have always been fascinated with vampires. Many of my favorite movies are about them. Throw witches into the cauldron and it takes these stories to a whole new level.

Thank you again to my friend, Michelle, for asking me to write a tale of best friend witches with vampire boyfriends. "Falling for Fangs" was only the beginning.

Another big thanks to Marita Woywod Crandle for writing the inspiring book "New Orleans Vampires: History and Legends". She also graciously gave me her permission to mention Boutique du Vampyre and Potions Lounge in "Falling for Fangs" and agreed to being an even bigger character in "Romance & Vampires" and "Make Me Immortal."

This tale may be good, but it wouldn't be great without the best editor on the planet, Brandi Zelenka. And cover designer Angela Haddon worked absolute magic!

Finally, love and thanks always to my family who provide never ending support. XOXO

About the Author

Ginger Lee, romance novelist and dark poet, spends her days raising her daughter, traveling with her husband, and attending concerts with friends. She is an avid reader and coffee & vampire enthusiast who collects art, movies, Monster High Dolls and oddities. In her free time, she enjoys walks through the neighborhood, thrift store shopping and watching Sanditon. Ginger loves to connect with other authors/readers and the writing community on social media.

Monsters (Inside of Us)

Big thanks to Missio for allowing me to share the lyrics to this song that has become the theme song of my vampire series.

Monsters (Inside of Us)
Song by Missio

I know you inside & out
Yes, I know you we met in my dreams
You can't fool me your heart is too kind
Think you're a monster
You must not know me
My heart is black as can be
Your heart is brighter than the sun
My body hangs from the rope
Your body lays gently in sleep
You're not a monster
I'm not a monster
But we have monsters inside of us
You're not a monster
I'm not a monster
But we have monsters inside of us
I'm tired of endless decay
You're tired of being alone

One day I'll kiss you goodnight
One day you will sing me to rest
You're not a monster
I'm not a monster
But we have monsters inside of us
You're not a monster
I'm not a monster
But we have monsters inside of us

How to Contact Ginger Lee

- Email: gleewrites@gmail.com
- Website: gleewrites.com
- www.twitter.com/glee_writes
- www.instagram.com/authorgingerlee
- https://ko-fi.com/gingerlee
- https://allauthor.com/author/gleewrites/.
- www.goodreads.com/gleewrites
- www.facebook.com/gingerweather
- Amazon:

www.ingramcontent.com/pod-product-compliance
Lightning Source LLC
Chambersburg PA
CBHW060230180626
46813CB00007B/3028